Shahzar
Warrior Queen

By Anastasia Rabiyah

Book One

Shahzar Book One: Warrior Queen

ANASTASIA RABIYAH

Copyright © 2007

Cover Art by ANASTASIA RABIYAH © 2007

Edited by D. THOMAS-JERLO-No Copyright Assigned

ISBN: 978-0-6151-6812-8

Published by Rabiyah Books, SEPTEMBER 2007

RabiyahBooks.com

Dedicated to: Fernando in Spain for his encouragement, Dawne' Dominique, Cynthia Moore, Caliope, Rachel and every Aspiring author who helped me in The Fantasy Novel Workshop.

Also to my family for their guidance, patience and love.

Table of Contents

Prologue

Raynier crossed the worship hall, his small, brown fingers tracing each bench. He heard his father's voice mingled with the bishop's as the two spoke at the side of a marble altar. Walking to the rear of the hall, he poked his head through an open doorway. Books, old, worn and stacked across shelves that lined the chamber beckoned to him. Curiosity made his small lips curl into a smile, an expression Raynier had not made since the last night he saw his mother. He took a seat at the long table centering the room and opened an ancient, fat tome. His fingers traced the words of the Shan-Sei religion's beginnings. He sounded out each letter as his mother had taught him, an unusual lesson for the child of a goat herder. She had wished for more than a simple life for her only son.

"A star sped across the heavens and rent the air with a crackling sound. Each of the three prophets looked up in time to see the full, blue moon come apart. Fire lit up the sky and pieces scattered across the heavens.

One bright light hurtled down from the remaining thirds of the moon. The prophets watched the fiery tail of the comet streak across the azure sky. Not far from where they stood, the piece of heaven met their planet's surface.

"Zafir, Hadi and Kateb found the blackened crater. Stumps of trees, still smoking, stood in a charred circle the size of a chieftain's tent. The forest bore its injury from the heavenly fall with a misty haze of smoke and steam. Each prophet crossed into that black circle and gave pause at what lay in its center.

"A woman's body, copper-skinned and blackened in patches from the fires, lay limp on the ground before them. They took her up and carried the fallen goddess to their tent and tended to her. The prophets offered her their bedrolls and fed her from their stores of food.

"Her eyes shone with the white light of dawn. 'I am Ishas,' she told the prophets. 'I have fallen from the heavens after chasing my lover for eons. My soul longs for rest among your kind. By dawn, my body will become ash. Bury what remains of me, and build a shrine in my honor. I am now your goddess. You three will be my prophets. All that spring from your seed will command the elements so long as they are beholden to me. My fire is nearly burned down.'

"Zafir, Hadi and Kateb watched over her through the night. As the sun's rays lit up their tent, the light reached across the rug for her outstretched fingers. Ishas spoke once more. 'Tell your people that I will rise again when the time is right. Do not let them forget me.'"

Raynier cringed when his father's hands clutched his shoulders, interrupting his reading. "It's time for me to go now, son."

The young boy looked up and saw tears in the older man's brown eyes. His dark, sun-weathered face twisted with sorrow. "Will I see you again, Father?" Raynier asked as he closed the delicate, old tome.

"No. You will not. Bishop Toman is your guardian now. Do all that he asks. Be obedient and loyal to him and his cause." With that, Raynier's father took his leave and walked out of his son's life forever. Raynier watched him go, longing to hug his father a final time and feel the itchy, wool of his patched tunic press against his face.

Moments later, Bishop Toman came for the boy. He smiled down at Raynier and held out his hand. Raynier could not help but stare at the kind-looking man. Toman appeared important in his black robes, his hair bound by an earth-colored turban and his waist tied with the same fabric. Raynier touched his guardian's fingers with reverence. The gentle bishop took the chain from his own neck and placed it over Raynier's head. "May you follow the light of Ishas all of your days," Toman said.

Raynier glanced down at the copper-colored talisman he now wore. Its shape reminded him of his mother when she would undress in the tent before bed. *I miss Mama,* he thought, for she had disappeared from his life along with the gentle cadence of bedtime stories and practicing letters in the sand. The young boy let his fingers clutch the charm, and an unsettling tingle passed through his body.

Chapter One: The Child

Shahzar stood beside her uncle Shahmi, a man she thought of as her father. She clung to his gray pant leg while the Kaladian council sentenced her to change that fact. The thin, little girl felt lost in the fierce looking man's shadow. Shahmi stood taller than most men, his leathery, brown skin darkened by days spent hunting Klemish raiders, and his body marred with battle scars. Shahzar stood beside him, feeling too young and innocent, her eyes wide as she waited to hear what the council would force her into next. The air in the large, circular council chamber smelled of parchment and fresh ink. Intricate, embroidered tapestries hung behind each council member, emblazoned with a symbol of their guild. Their rainbow colors and bold symbolism made her dizzy. The sunlight shining through the thick ceiling glass brightened the scene. She pushed a ringlet of her ebony hair back from her shoulder, already nervous. *I will not accept him.*

Sheah, the Speaker of the council, rapped her stick on the thick table to catch the attention of the other members. Most were huddled over their scrolls studying the agenda for the meeting. The council members paid little heed to her because her presence represented nothing but an old formality. Each turned to focus on the Speaker, whose voice echoed in the round room. The tiled floor helped to strengthen the sound.

"The first matter," Sheah said as she swept her thick braid over her shoulder. "Is Princess Shahzar's training, to allow her to take her place in this council."

The young princess turned to focus on Sheah's flowing, blue gown, as she spoke in a clear, yet dull voice. Sheah appeared too thick, more like the cooks from the kitchen than a leader. Shahzar studied the Speaker. She paid attention, knowing her place well because Uncle Shahmi explained it many times. *I will not be just another member,* she thought, *I will be queen.*

"After the meeting, you will be taken down to the Shan-Sei temple to meet your father." Sheah looked directly at Shahzar and smiled, "the Bishop Toman. Then you will begin your classes here in the castle." She fingered her twisted, ceremonial stick, clearly waiting for the princess's response.

Shahzar frowned. *Father,* she thought. *The bishop has never been my father, and he never will be.* Her tiny hand fell away from her uncle's pants. She clenched her fingers into fists while she looked past the Speaker, trying to contain her anger. The tapestry behind Sheah depicted Kah-Teth, the book of knowledge, in a vibrant display of rainbow colors. She tried to focus on the gold floss that made up the first few words of the book, but her temper got the better of her.

"Each of you will become her teachers and train her in the matters of your guild," Sheah continued. "She'll need to understand the importance of what you represent and the workings of all aspects regarding our great city."

Someone coughed, drawing Shahzar's attention from the tapestry. She noticed a few of the council members staring directly at her, their eyes reflecting boredom. *Toman isn't my father. If I meant anything to him, he'd have asked to see me before now.* The princess cleared her throat. "I won't see him!" she shouted. She stamped her foot against the tiles.

Sheah dropped her stick on the table, taken aback by the child's outburst. The others gasped, or at least turned to watch with more interest than before.

"He hasn't wanted to see me my whole life! Why should he be allowed to see me now?"

Shahmi's rough hand gripped her shoulder, but she didn't look up at him. She knew he hated the Shan-Sei temple. He wouldn't stop her. They were sentencing her to accept the bishop, a man she'd never known, a stranger that hid in the cursed, domed temple beyond the palace walls. She wouldn't do it. Already, she underwent tedious Traditions classes on etiquette and subservience, classes clearly meant to drain her budding will. "I refuse to see him! He should be put to *death!*"

The council members gawked, waiting for a resolution to the strange outburst. Shahzar knew what they thought; they could not afford for her to grow into her title and take away the power they all held. *I'll do it, though. I'll change everything about this council, all these stupid traditions.*

"That's enough, Shahzar," her uncle grumbled.

He pushed her away from the table, and she took the hint, stomping for the door. The young princess ran down the arched halls, angry with them all. She found the steps to the soldier's barracks and took them at top speed. Counting the doors, she dipped into her uncle's room. Shahzar hid in the back of the simple chamber and stared up at *the painting*. The woman posing in it looked young, beautiful, and frightened. A golden veil hid her hair, and layers of embroidered silk shrouded her body. She believed, by the way the woman's dark eyes gazed down from that canvas, her soul appeared hidden too. The painting, a rendering of Shahzar's mother, the former queen, entranced her. She sat down at the edge of her uncle's bed to wait for him, wishing the painting could speak.

Not long after, Shahmi burst in. He unbuckled his belt and tossed his weapons onto the dented, wooden table where they clattered before coming to rest. He tore away his sweaty, ash-colored tunic and frowned at his niece, an expression that made his leathery, brown face frightening.

Shahzar twisted her black hair around her fingers and fixed Shahmi with a serious gaze. "Please Uncle, tell me of my mother."

Shahmi's frown deepened, and that familiar sparkle of pain shone in his ebony eyes. He silenced her with his upraised hand. "You know what happened to her." Shahmi slumped in the only chair the room held. He scooted it closer to the table, sucked in a long, tired breath and let it out equally slow. Her uncle drew out his stone and rubbed oil on the surface. "My sister died birthing you. She died because of the temple and the old traditions. No queen takes the throne until she births a child blessed by the temple, a child sired by the bishop." Shahmi stole a glance at the painting. He dragged his dagger across the stone, his jaw tightening. "You should have gone to see him, Shahzar. You made a spectacle of yourself."

"I'm sorry, Uncle. It's just that..." She glanced over her shoulder at the painting. It too seemed to reproach her for her foul temper.

Shahmi stared at her, drawing the blade back and forth in measured strokes. "What? You think things can change?"

"No," she choked out, though she wanted to scream the opposite. Her uncle's serious face always stopped her from saying what she meant. She didn't fear him, but she didn't want to disappoint him either.

"You scared them, Shahzar." He shook his head, negating her outburst in the meeting. "You'll pay for that soon enough. The council has ruled with a strong hand since my sister's death." The dagger slipped across the stone, glittering from the light cast by the oil lamp on her uncle's table.

Shahzar pushed up from the bed, feeling smaller somehow.

"They don't want some little girl ordering death sentences, much less one that will be queen and able to force her whims to be carried out."

The constant swish-slide of the blade comforted her. It was a steady sound she'd grown used to. Shahzar admired Shahmi. He embodied everything she wanted to be: strong, stubborn and undefeatable. "I'm sorry, Uncle," she whispered. She stood up and tossed her hair back.

"Your first class is with Eschelle, the water guildmaster. After that, it's Horlan and then Yashpal. You know the way. I suggest you get going." He held up his dagger, studying the edge for any flaw.

"Yes, Uncle," she muttered. Shahzar touched his shoulder, and he cringed. She drew her hand away, bothered by his coldness when she attempted to show her affection.

Shahmi looked up at the painting of his sister. He pursed his thin lips and ran his fingers through his shorn hair. "Get going, girl. I'll see you this evening."

Winding her way through the halls, she passed under several archways without bothering to look at the paintings along the walls. She'd seen them countless times and their pastoral scenes seemed places of fantasy to Shahzar. Such green meadows and thick trees with myriads of leaves just couldn't possibly exist, she decided.

Eschelle waited for Shahzar behind the long table in her study. The tall, sturdy woman stood, garbed in a gold-colored dress that clung to her figure. She stared down her sharp nose and thrummed her thin fingers over the wood, eyeing Shahzar. The princess sat down and swallowed back her fear.

"You're late," Eschelle barked.

"I'm sorry," Shahzar murmured. The narrow study room felt cluttered. Paper diagrams of Kaladia's underground canals and aqueducts crisscrossed the walls. Bottled samples of water sat lined up on the table between teacher and student. She looked down at her dark hands and waited.

Eschelle slid the first sample across the table so it stood inches from Shahzar's fingers. Algae floated in the murky water, twisting round from the sudden movement. "Drink," the guildmaster ordered.

Shahzar opened her mouth to argue even though she knew she'd be defeated. She held the bottle to her lips, closed her eyes and swallowed. It went down thick, and left a rancid taste across her tongue.

"The algae adds to the flavor, making it seem foul when actually that sample is palatable," Eschelle explained. "You understand the meaning of that word, child?"

She felt afraid to answer. Weakly, she shook her head, no.

"Palatable means if you drink it, you won't die." Eschelle stood up straight, a proud aura gathering around her. "My people will never be forced to drink foul water. I take what I do seriously. That is to say, the water in my canals is pure."

"Palatable," Shahzar repeated. "I understand."

Eschelle pushed another bottle toward the child. The guildmaster's face dropped into a cold mask. Shahzar looked at the bottle and swallowed the lump in her throat. It had silt in it, bits of sand and muck. "And this one? Is it palatable?"

"Drink," Eschelle ordered again. "And you tell me."

"Y-y-yes, Mistress." She grasped the bottle and lifted it to her lips. The smell reminded her of the gardens. Closing her eyes, she took a swift draught and swallowed.

"Not the best?" Eschelle pondered aloud. "Not something you'd want to drink with the evening meal?"

"No, Mistress," Shahzar choked out.

Eschelle sneered. "Good, good. You're a fast learner." She swept her veil over her shoulder and sat down, pushing the next sample forward. Shahzar hated the torture, the uncertainty, but she endured it. After an hour of sampling fetid water from several sections of the city, she had a clear view of what palatable water should look and taste like.

Eschelle narrowed her eyes, a satisfied smirk on her painted lips. Even at such a young age, the princess could tell the lanky woman enjoyed feeling superior. Water meant life in the desert city, a commodity more valuable than coin. Eschelle reeked of self-importance. Shahzar watched the woman's long fingers curl around one of the bottles. Every digit bore a gem-filled ring. Bangles tinkled on her wrists when she held the bottle up and spoke. "Don't be late next time," she warned. "I won't tolerate it."

"Yes, Mistress," Shahzar mumbled. She scooted her chair out and backed her way to the exit. It would be a long day. She moped in the halls for a time before starting for Horlan's class.

Shahzar arrived early, before the sound of the hourly bell and sat at the small desk, waiting for Master Horlan. The study room resembled Eschelle's except that its large, arched window faced the domed gardens. Potted plants lined one side of the room, while the opposite wall housed a soil-less garden.

The old man burst through the door. Shahzar crinkled her nose at him. He was gray, balding, wrinkled and mean-looking. The lesson began with botanical names. Master Horlan hovered over her. She focused on his fingernails. Encrusted beneath each square-shaped nail was a black line of dirt.

"Ortis-nerephi," she repeated after him.

"And Phenellsian Perth, first cultivated in Shan-Sei for use in soaps," he wheezed out.

"Phenell…" she began, stumbling over the word. His gnarled fingers flew through the air as he slapped her cheek. Shahzar sucked in a startled breath. No one had ever hit her before.

"Again!" Horlan shouted. He moved against her desk, his earth colored tunic creasing where it met the wood. His hand stood at the ready to deliver another blow.

"Phenellsian Perth," she repeated in a shaky voice.

"What is it cultivated for?" His face shriveled. Horlan bent closer and she could smell his sour breath. He seemed to want her to fail.

"Soap." She feared meeting his gaze. He loomed like a wicked, desert wraith, a myth her dressing maid spoke of once. Horlan's gnarled fingers and scrawny forearms resembled Shahzar's vision of the monster.

"Kathcor beans." He fished in his pocket and dropped a handful of the pods in front of her. Their husks were still green at the tips.

"K-k-kathcor beans," she stuttered.

"Speak clearly!" Horlan produced a dried piece of cane and whacked her across the forearm once with it. "You may not think these things are important, that the plants we harvest and sow have any meaning." He leaned over her, and she bit her bottom lip to keep from crying. "But you're wrong!" he shrieked.

By the end of that hour-long lesson, she was crying. When he dismissed her, she ran from Horlan's study and hid in the shadows of an arch in the old hall. Shahzar wiped her face on her sleeves, staining the red fabric with wet splotches. Her cheek felt tender, and she flinched when she drew her sleeve across it too hard. With one more class left to attend,

Shahzar leaned against the thick wall and choked back her tears. *One more then it will be over for the day. Only one more,* she reminded herself. *I can do this.*

Yashpal, a tall man in his late forties, had dull, black eyes and a round belly that hung over his belt, barely disguised by his full, ash-colored robes. Shahzar entered his study and immediately covered her nose and mouth with her hand to stifle the odor. The room looked plain. No charts or maps hung from the walls. He turned when she approached, his round face stern. No chairs offered the young princess a place to sit. Her brow furrowed.

"Come, come, Princess," he said waving her over to where he stood. At the rear of the room beneath an open, arched window, there were three crates of refuse. "As you know, I am responsible for the waste our city generates."

Shahzar's eyes widened when she peered inside the first crate. Bloodied gobbets of meat and entrails filled it. They were rancid. In her seven years of life, she could not remember seeing anything so revolting.

"That," Yashpal said as he tapped the edge of the wood, "is true waste. Not much we can do except bury it." His pudgy fingers caught her by the wrist. He guided her to the next bin. "But this is different."

Shahzar leaned over and looked inside. Cayobac nut hulls and rinds from fruit were intermingled with spent leaves from the kitchens and gardens. At least the smell of that pile wasn't as nauseating.

"My guild turns this into soil for Master Horlan," Yashpal said.

At the mention of Horlan's name, she winced.

Yashpal caught the motion and let go of her wrist. His thick brows slowly formed a hairy frown. "Shahzar?"

She looked up into his twilight eyes and sensed less harshness than her first two teachers. When he started to kneel to her level, Shahzar took a step back, startled. "It's nothing, Master Yashpal."

His round finger tested the blazing skin on her cheek. He reached down and pushed up one of her sleeves. His gaze flashed over the bright, red lines across her coppery skin. "Hmm." Yashpal let the fabric fall back into place and stood up straight again. He rubbed the sides of his rotund belly and squinted at the wall. "That kind of 'nothing' teaches you to hate. They should know better. You will be queen one day." He turned his back on her, his face twisted with compassion. "Don't forget that, little one."

Shahzar felt more at ease in the presence of the imposing man. She began to forget the rank smell in the crate and started for the third one. "Please, Master," she said. "Continue with the lesson. I...I want to learn."

Yashpal nodded and bent over the next container of garbage. "This came from Rond's guild. He's kind enough to have it brought to my yards every morning."

Shahzar tried not to breathe too deeply. "Is it from goats?"

"Yes, yes. Sheep and goats. Sometimes it comes mixed with dung from the chickens and geese. Fine material for Horlan's gardens when composted properly, of course. You see, over time it degrades; it breaks down into something less vile. The plants take up the good parts of it and grow bigger than they would have without it. One thing you'll learn from me, little princess, is that nothing should be wasted. Not even the smallest of castoffs." Yashpal winked at her and Shahzar nodded, taking his meaning.

When she went to leave his class, he followed her to the door and rested a pudgy hand on her shoulder. "My advice, little one, is that you talk to your uncle about what happened today."

"It was nothing, Master," she said again, too afraid to say more.

"Yes, of course, nothing." He bent, glaring at the swelling mark on her cheek. "Listen to me, Shahzar. Tomorrow, in your classes with Vasuman and Jaider, do your best to remain silent. They'll find no fault in you so long as you let them breathe out their long-winded speeches and rants."

Shahzar met his eyes. "Thank you, Master."

He tapped her shoulder and smiled, revealing his crooked, yellow teeth. "Be wary of Machial," he warned. "Sheah will only want you to read. Our speaker craves knowledge and falls for any that feel the same. Read all she gives you. Ask for more. You must never tire of knowledge, little one. Always ask why," he cleared his throat, "just not from Eschelle or Horlan. The others aren't as harsh. They're too new to the council, but in time, they'll harden. And tell your uncle about the 'nothing'. Promise me."

"Yes, Master Yashpal," she whispered.

"Get along then, my little princess. I'll see you again in two day's time. Wear something less," he cleared his throat thinking of the right words. "Well, something you don't mind getting dirty. I want to take you to the fields."

Shahzar bit at her bottom lip, not fully understanding what the fields were, but ready to comply. She smiled at Yashpal and left, relieved the day's lessons had come to an end.

That evening, Shahzar waited in her uncle's room again. As always, the rustle of his buckle and the clatter of his two swords and countless daggers when he came in made her shuffle to the side of the bed. She watched him pull off his padded tunic and toss it over the chair. He turned on her and shook his head. Shahmi gave her a dark look, but she knew him well enough; he was glad not to be alone. "How did it go?" he asked.

The little princess pushed up her long sleeves. She held up her arms, brandishing her bruises, but Shahmi said nothing. The swelling of her cheek where Horlan had slapped her had not receded. Shahmi sighed and drew a blade. He oiled his stone and looked into it.

"Teach me to fight," Shahzar began, her voice cracking as the rage welled up. "Train me as a foot soldier!" The anger in her declaration startled both of them.

He raised his gaze from sharpening his favorite dagger. Their dark eyes met and he watched her long and hard in silence. His slow smile eased the tightness of his lips, and the scars about his face lessened in their harshness. "You?" Shahmi shot back as he placed the dagger in its sheath. "Did I hear you right? You wish to fight like the men?"

"A queen must be strong in all things her people are strong in, able to defend herself," she asserted.

Shahmi hissed through his teeth, a sound he often made when perturbed. "You want revenge." He returned his attention to his stone and drew another blade against it to make the steady swish-sliding sounds.

"Train me," she pleaded. "Every member of the council has been assigned to teach me except one. You."

"It's late and you should go back to your room. The council doesn't want you trained in such things. Much less, they don't want me present at their meetings. I may not be able to take the throne but by my blood relation to you, I still represent the royal family. That's something they'd like to be rid of. No royal family means the rule of Kaladia is theirs. They beat you in your classes today and will continue to do so until they break you."

Shahzar slipped off the bed and crossed the room. She watched the dagger slide against the stone, and her eyes welled with tears. "Please Uncle, don't let them."

The blade stopped. He looked at her, and she saw the cold in his deep, brownish-black eyes melting. "In the morning, come to the training field. I'll teach you. The council won't approve, but so long as you attend your other classes, they can't stop it."

That night when she crept into her oversized bed and stared up at the dull, green canopy, Shahzar decided she didn't want to be afraid. She pulled the covers up to her chin and winced at the pain in her arms. When she drifted to sleep, nightmares troubled her for the first time in her small span of life. Her hands and feet started to tingle; her body went cold. In her sleep, the little princess shivered.

Her dreams twisted. She felt the city around her, every small sound, each person walking along the cold, dark streets. Kaladia was alive and breathing all around her. Her heart raced and her mind touched on each of the four walls that bordered the city. Her vision traced the span of the second set of walls. Last, it settled in Kaladia's heart. There she felt the movements of the priests. Beneath their snores and the few that prayed to Ishas, she felt another presence, a small thing resting far below the building, a being she could not begin to fathom. Shahzar woke screaming.

Chapter Two: The Temple

Ten years slipped away, and the last day of the council's formal training passed. Shahzar stood in the courtyard outside the soldiers' barracks feeling anxious about her impending ascension to the throne and the rite it entailed. Torches lit the darkness in the circular practice area. The princess caught the hilt of her opponent's scimitar with hers and sent it flying to land in the dust nearby. Irlecain braced himself, his chest heaving for air beneath his ash-colored tunic.

She barreled into him, knocking Irlecain to the ground, her favored move. Shahzar used her lithe, muscular body to her advantage, though she stood a hand shorter than her opponent.

"Tomorrow," he managed, struggling for breath beneath her, "you'll go into that castle and never come back out. They'll make you sit by the fire and sew, growing fat and lazy with all their pomp."

"I'll be queen, and when I am, things will change," she spat as she seized his wrist and pressed it to the dusty earth. His other hand remained trapped between their bodies.

"You're a woman; you can't change things," he rasped. Irlecain seemed to like irritating her. He grinned and chuckled when she glared down at him.

Shahzar frowned, fury taking over. She pulled her dagger, and laid the blade against his forehead. "What did you say?"

"You heard me," he huffed, no fear shining back from his green eyes.

Her hand trembled then swiped. Shahzar pushed away from Irlecain, still glaring. Blood ran down the side of his face as he rose. Startled, he reached up and blotted at the injury. "Why did you do that?" he cried out.

"To teach you your place. The place of second, an underling to me."

"I thought we were friends, Shahzar." He pushed his palm against the cut and winced. "After all the times I stood by you against the raiders, all the times I told Sadot you really were a girl, not a boy with long hair." He chuckled again, still shocked, but taking the moment well. "What kind of person cuts her friend's face?"

Irlecain's insults were not unusual, but she felt edgy and impatient. "You deserved it. You know better than to push me." She wiped the dagger on her gray pants and pursed her lips.

Irlecain smiled wide, an expression that charmed most. "I'll miss you after today," he offered.

She returned his cocky grin. "You'll see me. If you outlive the raids, you may be Captain of the Guards one day." The princess paused as the bells announced the evening meal. Soldiers languishing by the barracks soon rushed past to make their way to the dining hall. The scent of roast lamb and turmeric wafted on the cool, desert breeze. "When Shahmi retires, that is."

"Shahmi will never retire. He'll spend his last hours in battle and so will I." Irlecain puffed out his chest, already too proud of his rank in the foot-soldiers. He grinned wider, bending to retrieve his scimitar and slide it back into its scabbard.

Their hands met, fingers curling around each other and they shook them together, a strange farewell for the two friends. After that night, she'd begin her journey to take the throne and fight for the power the council had taken. Irlecain, the best tracker in the army, would begin his training as an assassin and a spy. "You'll write to me from Bisura?"

"Every week." He smirked and held fast to her hand. "You should come with me. You're meant to kill, not sit on a throne." He nodded at the castle. "They wouldn't miss you."

"I don't think assassin's training will improve my methods." Shahzar pulled her hand away from his, frowning. She did want to go with him, for his company more than anything else. Irlecain matched her when they fought. They'd become a team, almost inseparable. It saddened her to part from him. "You write to me, and when you're done with your training, there's something I want you to find."

His brow rose, revealing his intrigue over a quest. "I'll find whatever you seek. You know that." He glanced over Shahzar's shoulder and nodded. No one watched them. The others had all gone to eat. He edged closer and held up his arms to embrace her. She cleared her throat and backed away. Irlecain let his hands fall to his sides. The awkward moment passed. "I'll write; I promise," he said. "Farewell, my princess." He spun on his heels, stalked toward the soldier's dining hall and disappeared.

-o.O.o-

In the morning, Shahmi came to his niece's room. He sat at the edge of the bed, picking at the velvet coverlet. Shahzar gazed up at him, love showing in her eyes but never spoken, as he requested, for such feelings, he warned, were only for those that desired ruin. She could tell he felt nervous by the way he avoided her gaze. The morning light showed through the window behind him, framing his stoic silhouette in gold.

Shahzar sat up, letting the jade-colored covers fall away and the chill in the air wake her. Her long, loose sleeping gown clung to her ankles as she wiggled her toes in the thick, green rug. She hadn't had any nightmares, so she wondered what ill news he'd come to relay. "What is it, Uncle?" she asked as she eyed him warily.

Shahmi ran his hand through his closely shorn hair, a gesture that often forewarned a great battle to come. "I'm to take you to the temple this day, Shahzar. The Bishop has announced his desire to go on a final hermitage."

"I've no wish to see him," she said, cutting her uncle off and mistaking where the conversation headed. "He ignored me for seven years. Let him go and die then." Her thoughts had not turned to Bishop Toman since that day in the council meeting so long ago.

"That's not why I'm to take you, Shahzar." Shahmi sighed and scrutinized her. "He's choosing a priest to succeed him. The new bishop will become the father of your child. Then, once the baby comes, you will be queen."

Shahzar waved her hand in disgust. "The Shan-Sei temple is a farce, a façade. I'm surprised the council let it stand this long. I'll bear no priest's child. The tradition is ridiculous."

Shahmi stood up, his dark eyes cold and troubled. "Then help end the temple, Shahzar," he whispered with desperation. "When he chooses his successor and the new priest comes to your bed, kill him."

With pursed lips, she gathered up the mass of her curly hair and twisted it round and round. The idea had its merits. *The temple offers nothing to the city in return for its existence and the tithes the citizens pay. However,* she wondered. *Why all the fear of the place, of its mystical powers?* She'd seen nothing convincing her that any such dark power, as the council often referred to it, even existed. The vengeance in her uncle's voice intrigued her, and she wanted to please him. "Let us go there now!"

Not long after, dressed and primped befitting her station, Shahzar followed Shahmi down the castle's marble steps. Guards marched in time at her sides and back, though she thought them unnecessary. As they crossed the brick road that led to the temple of Shan-Sei, she inclined her gaze to study the building. Behind her, the merchants called out to the townspeople. A small herd of goats crossed the road and dipped into the alley, followed by a scrawny, old man. A high wall, muraled in tiles, surrounded the temple. The early morning sun glittered against the pieces of baked clay and glass, making it appear much more substantial than it was. Beyond the wall, there were four thin, high minarets. The top of the central dome, which housed the circle room, rose as a bulbous beacon to the heavens. The temple needed new paint; the teal color showed patchy in many places and peeling in others.

Her entourage passed through the open gates and into the courtyard. When she stepped into the dust-covered area littered with stacks of rushes and filled with the noise of dogs, Shahzar felt shocked by how simply the priests lived. *This is what the council speaks of? This filthy, ill-kempt, run-down place? What power could possibly cling to such a building?*

The dogs in the courtyard smelled bad. They lunged at the princess, snapping and growling at the new intruder. Shahmi grunted when one broke loose, making for Shahzar's dress. She snatched it by the throat and glared at the beast. The animal yelped in pain. Its master came running toward the entourage and tied the dog back with the others.

Shahzar looked the man up and down. He stood dressed, as all the priests, in black robes with a brown silk belt, his head wrapped in a matching brown turban. The heat of the day made Shahzar wonder what fool had come up with such attire in the midst of a desert city. It led her to believe the priests spent most of their time indoors.

"Princess," he said as he held out his sweaty hand. "I am Endela, the bishop's high priest. Your presence here, at this early hour is...unexpected." He gazed past her, his beady eyes filled with questions. "May I lead you to the circle within the temple? Bishop Toman is there. I am certain he will be elated to see you."

"Yes, and I'll come alone," she said.

Her uncle's lips pursed, but he stayed where he was. The guards, accustomed to her ways, also remained.

"Oh, that's not necessary," Endela began. His eyes shifted from Shahzar to her chaperone, as if she shouldn't be the one to decide where to go alone.

In that instant, she decided she didn't like the man. He looked mousy with his long nose and straight, dark line of a brow shading his small, sparkly eyes. Though the heat felt stifling, she decided he looked too sweaty, a side effect of nervousness.

At last, Endela turned, muddled, and led her past cracked arches and plastered halls deep into the heart of the temple. Windows set into the walls of the round central building let in light. Endela and the princess passed one and she narrowed her eyes to look inside. She could see an old man sitting on the rug. Beside him was another, younger priest that blatantly stared back at her. His gaze startled her and she smiled. He seemed frozen, without emotion, a dark, shadowy sculpture behind glass.

Endela went through the oaken door and latched it shut. Shahzar tapped her foot as she waited outside, listening while he announced her unexpected arrival.

"She wishes to see you," came Endela's high, screechy voice. "Yes, alone. She said her uncle must wait in the courtyard." The bishop's voice carried too softly to make out. Shahzar edged closer, curious, for the first time, about the stranger that sired her.

The door creaked open. She glared at the mousy advisor. "Leave," she commanded. "I wish to speak to Bishop Toman."

Endela squeaked in protest.

"Get out!" She growled at the meek, little priest.

The bishop nodded and Endela scuttled off. Shahzar strode into the circle room. The tapestries disturbed her. They presented the whole Division of Shan-Sei. Boldly embroidered images glared accusingly at her in bloody reds, fiery oranges and crisp greens. She paused to study them, for although they were aged, they'd been well cared for. Having attempted the sewing duties Irlecain warned her of, she appreciated their craftsmanship. Candles, as well as the sunlight from the open windows, lighted the circle room. It smelled musty, the scents of melting wax and smokewood incense lingering in the air. The faded carpet, ancient and well-worn, bore the two seated men. Bishop Toman and the other priest were side by side, appearing as equals.

Shahzar crossed the distance to the priests with poise and dignity. She held her head high and kept her shoulders back. The princess knelt before Toman and stared into his pale, clouded eyes, wondering if he could even see her. He appeared to be blind.

"Shahmi just informed me that my children will be fathered by the next bishop," she spat. She refused to start any small talk with Toman because she had no wish to know him. Coming to the temple and facing the old man proved a new challenge for her.

"Yes, Daughter, that's the way of the Shan-Sei," Bishop Toman replied, his small mouth quivering.

The other priest gasped and Shahzar assumed he did so because of Toman's use of the word daughter. She belonged to the castle, not to Toman and tradition forbade the use of such an endearment. Shahzar's attention stayed on the Bishop though, his old, wrinkled face and his murky pupils.

"This city is no longer called Shan-Sei." Shahzar leaned forward, placing one hand on the aged carpet. "It's changed since the Division and will continue to change, as I will it. Where is the new bishop?"

Toman's cloudy pupils sought out the priest sitting next to him then again tried to return to Shahzar. He paused, his wrinkle-lined, brown face creasing as he concentrated. "There are three candidates, and I haven't chosen which will succeed me."

Shahzar turned to the other priest, wondering why Toman had done so. The priest still gazed at her intently, and it made her feel uncomfortable. "Why are you here?" she asked, raising her voice.

Toman's thin lips pressed together. He spoke with quiet anger. "You're spoiled and willful. You have no manners. You shame your mother's good name."

She ignored the old man, her gaze still fixed on the priest. "Well?"

"I'm here to discuss the nominations with the bishop," he replied.

His deep brown eyes were magnificent. They seemed to exude depth and character she rarely saw in men. He looked calm, unhindered by her presence, though he watched her in a manner she couldn't describe. Shahzar nodded, and felt his eyes still on her as she returned her attention to the bishop.

"I didn't know my mother. She died birthing me. I don't know you because your traditions required that I not until my seventh year. When the council tried to force me to meet with you, I denied them. If my own father wouldn't want to see me for seven years then why should he see me at all? I doubt, even now, that you can see me. If I shame my mother's good name, then I shame yours as well. You've no right to condemn my manner. I'll be queen of this city. You'll die in your hermitage, cold and alone."

"You will be queen, Shahzar, when you have born a child blessed by the temple." The bishop's old voice remained steady. His dark hands lay in his lap, and she saw them move toward her.

"Then the tradition will stand?" she asked, anger stifling her voice.

"As it has since the Division." Toman closed his eyes against her. His fingers curled as he balled his hands up. The bishop leaned back on his heels and swallowed hard. He looked like he would cry.

"We shall see." She stood, matter-of-factly. "Inform me when you have ordained the new bishop. I'll keep with your little tradition, sick as it is." Shahzar turned to the priest and found he still watched her, unashamed to stare. She felt he wanted to tell her something, but his lips remained set.

"When I am Queen, I shall abolish these traditions. I'll bring this city into its former glory once more. I'll stop the raids from Klem. I'll be the most powerful queen Kaladia has ever had."

Toman raised his face, his clouded pupils struggling to meet her gaze. "I have no doubt that you speak the truth, Daughter."

She left the room with a last backward glance at the younger priest flanking Toman. Still he stared at her, his face tight with an expression she finally likened to wonder. The priest wore the same black robes, brown silky belt and turban they all did. He looked like any other Shan-Sei. A man, she decided, of little consequence.

Chapter Three: Tustin

The rains spread north across the wastelands, soaking the dunes and filling the wells along the seldom-used trade routes. The element followed a calling, a path to a thirsty city. Caravans from the forestlands no longer came so far, unwilling to risk the arduous journey for the sake of spices, weavings and exotic fabrics they could easily get in Kaladia. Two generations ago, after the Division, the Klemish faction fled Shan-Sei to make their own city. The massive settlement rose from the barren desert in shades of gray and black, a result of the stones mined in the Goadhiri quarry over which the Klemish founded their great city. It mimicked the shape of Kaladia, bearing two walls. The first, upon approaching it, stood so high that a man would have to tilt his head precariously back to see its crenellated top. Archers patrolled the wall in ordered lines. Klem's forged gates lay open because they had no enemy willing to raid their borders. Like the forestland traders, even the Kaladians had no desire to make the journey.

In the blackened castle that centered the bustling city, Riel, the high guard cringed as the city's king, Tustin Aberweir, laced his fingers together and leaned forward. Tustin rested his joined hands on the ebony table in one of his many meeting rooms. The Klemish king looked impressive in his azure cloak and gold tunic. The blazon across his chest, an amethyst dragon's face with a flaring red mane, glared at the man seated across from him. Tustin narrowed his cold, smoldering eyes on Riel. "These raids mean nothing," the king said, arching one brow. "You take their livestock, kill a few people. How does this help my cause?" The oil lamp flickered, distorting the fierce king's startling face.

Tustin's brother, Dalin Fah, rubbed his chin in earnest, waiting to hear what Riel would offer. The brothers looked like twins. Both bore the same long topknot on an otherwise shaved head. Tattoos scarred each man's face, although Tustin's were the more legitimate. He'd received them when he married into royalty eleven years ago, not long after his failed attempt to kill Ashandera, his naïve bride. Dalin mimicked all his older brother did, down to the tattoos and the violent hatred for Kaladia.

Riel swept his fingers across his sweaty brow. "My king, if you want the troops to do more, you have only to order it. Your will is mine."

Tustin slammed his fist against the ebony wood and snarled. "Of course I want more! I want the city! I want the Shan-Sei temple burned, the Kaladian council slaughtered and that child of a princess cut down before she grows into her throne!"

Dalin nodded at Riel, seconding his brother's wishes. He leaned forward, a mirror image of the king, his clothes reflecting his worship for his brother. They matched Tustin's in style if not in exact color. Riel knew he needed to choose his words carefully, for at any moment the double pair of feral, black eyes might want to see the captain dead.

"I will gather the troops, my king, and have them march on Kaladia at dawn," Riel offered in a quavering voice.

"A siege?" Dalin gasped out.

Tustin turned on his doting brother and shook his head, silencing the man. His fist, still balled atop the dark wood, slowly unfurled. Riel let his hands fall to the side, out of sight, all the better to appear submissive. He looked between the brothers at the mural of Daumion, the dragon-god of Klem. It spanned the wall in a shiny, tiled display, its mismatched eyes watching the captain with hunger.

"A siege is a fool's move, Riel. Kaladia has two walls. The first is near impenetrable. The days of honor against our enemy are over. Where was the honor in casting the Klemish faction out? Where was the honor in razing the forest, leaving us to subsist in this?" He raised his arms out, indicating the sandy wastes that surrounded Klem. "The Kaladians deserve no mercy, no honor."

Riel cleared his throat. He looked down at the papers strewn over the meeting table and worried. Something terrible would happen. He knew the cold look in Tustin's eyes. The king already had a plan. This interrogation must be a formality to show his power. The captain knew better than to argue. He swallowed back his fear. "What do you suggest, my king?"

"Round up the mercenaries from the south quarter. I want men without inhibition, killers that won't question my orders. I can pay them well enough." Tustin stood up, signifying a quick end to the proceedings. "I don't want any of my wife's loyalists fouling my plans. We'll leave at dawn, but not for a siege."

Riel stood too. He wiped his sweaty palms on the hem of his azure uniform, feeling relieved. Tustin often killed those beneath him on a whim.

Riel felt lucky to have lasted three months longer than the last captain did, but he held no illusions about his own end. *I will die when he finds fault in me,* he thought. *That day is short in coming.* He bowed slightly. "It will be done, my King."

Dalin stood up too and pushed his chair beneath the table. He hurried to open the door for Tustin, his haunting eyes fixed on his brother. The three made their way down the arched hall. Riel watched the way ahead, his thoughts slipping into panic. *Mercenaries rather than the city's own soldiers? Tustin must be out of his mind.*

They walked in line down the tiled stairs and turned. Tustin led them past the queen's quarters. Riel spared a glance through the open doors and frowned at her. Cream-colored gauze curtains shrouded Ashandera's gilded bed, yet the captain saw her. She looked like death sitting up against the amethyst pillows with her eyes cast to the window and a mournful pout on her sunken face.

"Husband!" she called in a raspy voice. Tustin stopped and turned to regard her. Riel took a step back, waiting. Dalin actually moved toward the open room and leaned on the jamb to watch, his eyes shifting from king to queen.

"Our son wants to be let into the guard," Ashandera said. "He wants to fight alongside you." Slowly, her head turned and she pinned each man with a fierce look. Riel sucked in a breath. The woman should have died long ago. The little life left in her seemed to dwindle more each time he saw the queen. He knew why Tustin didn't finish her off. The king took pleasure in making others serve him. Those that didn't do so willingly, he maimed, tortured or deprived. Ashandera suffered in her forced illness, and Riel knew that gave Tustin reason enough to keep her. The ruler delighted in her weakness and his blatant ability to undermine her control over the city.

The king quirked his brow in reaction to his wife's announcement. "Lochnar told you this?" he called across the room. Riel sucked in a breath. The prince had always been a sinister child, given to killing birds. The captain remembered the first time he encountered the boy. Lochnar may have been five or six years old back then, but he'd possessed no youthful innocence. Riel found him just outside the hawk house, his small fists full of wing feathers. The king had raged over the death of his hunting birds, but Riel knew the twisted man took pride in his son's dark pursuits.

"Just this morning," Ashandera said, breathless. She pushed her body up, only a few inches higher, as if trying to see who else watched her from the hall. "I forbid it!"

Riel shook his head. The woman just wouldn't learn.

"Then I'll have him brought to the fields right now." A slick smile spread across Tustin's tattooed face. "Lochnar will be trained." He shook his finger at the queen. "You don't look well, woman. Better get some more rest. I wouldn't want you dying on me."

The anger shone in her brown, glittering eyes. Riel felt it, even across the room. Ashandera clenched the blanket in her hands, pursed her lips and turned back to the window.

Tustin shrugged and set off again down the hall. Dalin snickered at the queen, his eyes trained on her in a lustful way. Riel could only watch. What more was there to do? She never should have married such a vile man. The captain remembered his days in the lower ranks when Tustin Fah courted the young queen. He swindled her with his charms, kept his true self hidden until the wedding ended. Even Riel had heard the king boast about the poison, about the failed attempt on the queen's life so many years before.

Riel shook his head and followed the king. Some part of him felt sorry for Ashandera Aberweir. She'd married too young and never even tasted the power she inherited over Klem. Tustin stole it away and harbored it with a mindless greed. Riel caught up to the king at the end of the hall and fell in step, trying to avoid attention.

"Dalin!" Tustin yelled. "Get over here and quit gawking at my wife!" The king spun on his heels, a vicious snarl tainting his lips.

Riel stepped past Tustin. "I will gather the men for you," he murmured and rushed away. If the two fought, one might want a scapegoat, some unfortunate bystander. The captain didn't want that part.

He walked at a hurried pace, almost a run, heading for the barracks. The courtyard teemed with young soldiers. They practiced with rattan swords and woven shields, batting each other with loud cracking sounds. Riel crossed through their ranks, his eyes on the front of the blocky building that housed all the soldiers at night. The modest chambers could not compare to his private chattel closer to the inner gardens. That detail delighted his wife and comforted him when Tustin made Riel do things he did not agree with. The captain's higher pay proved worth the disloyalty to Queen Ashandera, he reminded himself, but he began to fear that his end would not.

Riel emerged in his cousin's modest room. He glanced around at the meager accommodations, a worn table, its leg crooked, a single chair and a wooden shelf lined with dog-eared books and piles of paper. The cabinet where D'atham kept his clothes was ajar, revealing the uniforms within. Riel didn't bother to sit down, but he did close the yellowed curtain over the single, arched window. "D'atham," he said, acknowledging the thick man who sat on a cot, meditating. "The king has ordered me to gather mercenaries for an attack on Kaladia."

D'atham's bald head lifted slowly. His kind, brown eyes caught on Riel, holding the man steady. He reached back with one hand to find his beige tunic. "Why?"

"Tustin sounds worse," Riel whispered. "He wants the Shan-Sei temple burned, the Kaladian council killed and their princess as well." He paced, his hands behind his back.

"Does the queen know of this?" D'atham's eyes rolled from side to side as he watched his cousin move. When Riel halted, D'atham pulled on his tunic and pushed up from the cot. He stretched, flexing the muscles that bulged across his arms.

Riel shook his head. He didn't know why he still told his cousin the king's plans. Maybe he felt sorry for his ill queen or maybe some part of him thought he could escape his ill-fated destiny. Riel knew Tustin Aberweir's path would end badly. Old hatred bred more hatred, and the king liked to kindle such feelings.

"You'll get them from the south quarter?" D'atham asked. He reached for his belt and strapped it on, his thick, meaty fingers deftly clasping the buckles.

"Cousin, what am I to do?" Riel heard the desperation in his own voice and he didn't care. There must be a way out other than death. His mind turned to his wife. He didn't want to make her a widow. He rubbed his forehead and stared plaintively at the muscular man in front of him. D'atham always knew what to do to make things right. He never wavered, never faltered and Riel regretted not having the same strength.

"The army belongs to the queen, not to Tustin. The city, the people, they are all wards of Ashandera." D'atham tightened his belt and frowned. "Tustin will drive Klem into the ground. He won't stop until every citizen able to bear arms sets out for revenge on a city that never attacks us."

"D'atham, what should I do?" Riel sighed and hoped for a solution. His cousin pulled on his jalail and laced it over his tunic. He held his arms out and surveyed the length of the sleeves. It weighed on Riel to watch his cousin thinking.

"You chose the path you're on, Riel," D'atham replied. "I can't make decisions for you. That you've come to me now leads me to believe you see the error of your ways. All I can do is inform the queen's advisors. Maybe Zodrian will have ideas on what to do. I follow my queen and you follow Tustin. That's the way of things." D'atham held his hand out and Riel took it. "Go round up his mercenaries. I hope you live through this."

Riel frowned, defeated. "And I you."

Chapter Four: The New Bishop

Shahzar pushed the needle through the muslin and pricked her thumb a third time. Aggravated, she growled and sucked away the blood. "Waste of time," she muttered as she stood and tossed the project into the palm-leaf basket by her cushioned seat. The other women looked up, their dark eyes the only visible part of their veiled faces. The light from the fire in the hearth cast a warm glow on her witnesses. Shahzar stormed out and slammed the door. She thought of Irlecain and how right he'd been. It soured her mood even more as she hurried down the arched halls, past the murals of the first queens and stomped up the marble stairs to her room.

"I hate this," she fumed as her squat servant, Inell, darted out of the princess's reach. Shahzar paced and finally stopped beside her desk. "I hate not being allowed in the fighting yards. I hate how they control me!" She slammed her fist against the wood. Onyx message sleeves rattled in protest.

Inell's eyes bulged. She normally took the brunt of Shahzar's anger and tried to remain calm. She set the day's scrolls on the pile at the corner of the desk and hurried to rearrange the curtains around the bed in a deft attempt to avoid her mistress.

Shahzar closed her eyes, thinking about the council meeting. That morning, Bishop Toman had chosen his successor. After a ceremony held on the outskirts of the city, he began his hermitage. In the meeting that followed, the council spoke against Shahzar's wish not to attend. She even voiced her blatant opinion, which startled them as it always did. "What do I care? The old fool wants to go off and die in the sands, then let him! I'm his daughter by circumstance. I feel nothing for him, nor do I want to," was her cool offering.

She shook her head, wondering if she should feel something for the old bishop. Her last chance to know him passed when his camel carried the nearly blind, old man into the wastelands.

"Are you ready to change now, milady?" Inell spoke in the softest way, ready to bolt if the princess lost her temper and decided to throw one of the onyx sleeves from her desk.

The selection of the new bishop meant that the night had finally come for him to enter her bedroom. The council wanted to make a production of it, a celebratory event. Her uncle stood for her and forbade it. He promised her that he would bring the priest discreetly up to her room with no pomp or fanfare.

"Yes," she answered, with a deep sigh. "Get me ready."

The servant helped Shahzar to undress. She folded up the soiled clothing and piled the bundle on the chair by the door. Inell returned to

Shahzar's side and pulled the ceremonial gauze dress over the princess. A taut thing it was, meant to accentuate her curves and tempt the bishop. Shahzar studied it in the polished, metal mirror, her face clearly echoing the rage in her heart. She went silent, letting her maid believe she would go through with the rite. *They all must believe or else Shahmi's plan won't work.*

Shahzar sat down at her desk while Inell unbraided the princess's hair. The servant ran a brush through the wavy, black mass, patiently straightening the curls. It was the one thing that could calm her. Shahzar leaned back and closed her eyes when Inell began to hum. An hour passed as she relaxed and let her mind become one with what she would do that night.

When, at last, the knock came, the princess took refuge within the curtains of her bed. She lay there, fingering the cold handle of her dagger beneath the pillow while Inell extinguished the oil lamps. The room was swathed in soft candlelight and new shadows danced across the thick walls.

Inell opened the door. "He is here, milady," she called. Her footsteps fell away as she descended the marble steps. The door clicked shut, and Shahzar was now alone with the new bishop.

Through a crack in the bed curtains, she watched him. He was rather tall, dark of skin and eyes, as most Kaladians were. His long, straight nose and small mouth gave him away. He was the same priest that had stared at her when she'd spoken with Toman. The new bishop stepped onto the green carpet and eyed it curiously. In fact, he studied everything about the ornate room with eyes too wide and frightened to warrant Shahzar's plans to kill him. She pulled her hand away from the hilt of her blade and pushed back the jade-colored, bed curtains.

He froze, his eyes trained on her dress. Shahzar stepped deliberately toward him, hoping he would bolt like a frightened animal. His expression led her to believe he would.

"You're early." She covered the distance between them in long, graceful steps.

"I'm sorry, Your Majesty. I can return again later if that is your wish." His soft tone held no air of self-importance.

"No. Better to be done with this." Shahzar stopped in front of him, thinking she must stick to the task at hand and not waver despite his magnificent eyes. He was a mere target, a device upon which to pinpoint and unleash her rage. She reached up and untwisted his russet-colored turban so that his hair fell down against his back. Color rose in his cheeks, and his breathing grew rapid. She touched the silver streaks among the dark strands.

"How old are you?" she asked, startling him further.

"Barely thirty."

"At thirty your hair is going gray?" She walked around him, surveying his form, the way he carried his weight. It was a habit she'd picked up in her training under Shahmi. Shahzar judged his weaknesses. "What's your name?"

"Bishop Raynier." He averted his eyes to the shadows moving beyond her desk in an obvious attempt to avoid looking at the curves of her body.

"I saw you that day in the temple. I remember you," she murmured accusingly. "You stared at me." Her manner softened because he looked away. She felt less of a target then.

"I didn't mean to offend you, Your Majesty," he said with sincerity.

She leaned close and stared into his eyes, drawing his attention. "Don't call me that. I'm Shahzar. Please, call me by my name. If we're in public, you may call me by my title. Here and when we speak privately, I am Shahzar. May I call you Raynier, or do you already cleave to your new title?"

"Raynier is fine." His breathing hastened.

"Are you in a hurry to be back to your temple, Raynier?" Her voice was quite calm. She felt satisfied to see a bead of sweat break upon his forehead.

"No." His amber brown eyes locked on hers.

"Mmm." Shahzar stepped back from him finally. The stray thought occurred to her that he could be useful if she let him live. It contradicted all her uncle had told her. "Let us speak frankly," she began, "now and in all things we discuss. We are to make a child. This isn't my choice. If I'm to be queen, then I must perform this task. I have but one hope in you, but I think my hope will be lost when you answer me this. Do you possess the dark power?" She pressed her luck by being so direct, crossing a taboo line.

His mouth gaped. "No, I do not!"

"Does any priest within the temple possess it?" She went on, ignoring his indignation. She had to know, had to be sure.

"It is forbidden."

"Then," she began as she turned from him. "It is as I feared." Shahzar went to her desk and glanced over the papers there, the countless scrolls, the onyx sleeves, the quills, the ink, all was in a state of turmoil. She liked it that way, though it bothered Inell. She liked it that way because it disturbed her so. Shahzar always felt Inell was spying, and so she forbade her to organize it. It was easy enough for the princess to find what she needed among the clutter.

She ran her forefinger over the curled parchment from Irlecain. He was in Binitha when he sent it, tracking down the old Shan-Sei, the priests that knew how to channel Ishas's energy, how to manipulate the dark power for their own causes. If any remained, she had faith he would locate them.

Shahzar faced Raynier, still unsure of what to do. She took in a deep breath and let it out in a sharp sigh. "Let's get this over with so you can return to your post and I can return to mine." It upset her to lead him on, but she needed the murder to look legitimate. Blood stains on the carpet instead of the bedsheets might cause questions in the morning. Shahzar closed her eyes tight for a moment and pushed away all emotion.

Rain began to drip against the arched window as clouds darkened the sky and the room in turn. The bishop stood frozen, staring, clearly disappointed and at a loss for words. Shahzar wondered if he could sense the change in her. The sky reflected her mood, the churning emotions that curdled in an unfamiliar place inside her.

She came to him and took his hand, struck by how warm it was in hers. He followed her to the bed and sat as she directed him. First, Shahzar knelt and pulled off his boots. She set them neatly by the bedpost. She unfastened his black robes. The bright light from the plethora of candles lit his bare chest. It was speckled with hairs, some gray and some dark. She studied them, memories of her uncle's battle-scarred chest tarrying in her thoughts. For a moment, her gaze caught on the amulet he wore. It was copper-colored, representing Ishas as a shapely woman with her arms upraised. Shahzar reached out to touch the holy talisman, but let her hand fall lower at the last second. Her fingers worked to untie his brown silk belt, her mind disconnected from the moment. Raynier breathed so fast that she felt it against the top of her head.

"Shahzar," he said, barely a voice in the word.

She glared up at him, wondering why she'd gone so far. "Why do you stare at me like that? What do you want from me?" He had that same look in his eyes, the one from the temple when she'd smiled at him through the window.

"I'm in love with you," he added in a breathless voice.

His silk belt drifted from her hand and whispered as it touched the carpet. His words stunned her. He seemed so relieved to have spoken them, but they tore at her heart. Mystified by his declaration, the princess stood and backed away. Her backside hit the edge of her desk and she stumbled.

The rain, such a rarity in Kaladia, turned angry. It beat at the stained glass in the arched window frame. Shahzar spun around and bent to light a candle on the desk, then another. Her hands shook. *This isn't going as planned,* she thought. *Rain should be a good omen. But it doesn't feel so.* Smoke drifted from the yellow flames in snaking tendrils. She ran out of candles to light.

Shahzar knew she had to end the moment, to kill him before her feelings took over. She'd never been nervous over the prospect of killing an enemy before. She didn't turn, refusing to look at him, trying to stay on track. "Go. Lie in my bed. Make it warm for me." Her voice sounded cold.

He climbed into the dark bed and slid under the soft, jade-colored coverlet without a word. She could hear him shuffling to the side and the sound of the pillows shifting. Shahzar waited until he stopped moving.

Just kill him. Even though she knew she must, the idea shamed her. He'd committed no crime. Killing Klemish raiders on the outskirts was one thing, but the bishop was Kaladian. It didn't feel right, especially after his strange confession. *I'm in love with you.* She clenched her hands into tight fists. *Is he mad?* Shahzar shook her head. *He doesn't even know me. It is impossible to feel something like that for a person you just met.*

She touched the edge of another scroll, one from the temple's records. It stated that the last known priest possessing the dark power was Al-Shing Ganeria Danton who'd left on hermitage over twenty years ago, long before her birth. She stared at the scroll. Rumors alleged Al-Shing went south into the forestlands, that he married a priestess from Edchir, but no one had heard from him in years. No sightings. Nothing. The trail was cold. Even the priestesses of Edchir had vanished. She closed her eyes when the coverlet rustled and wondered again what to do about the bishop. "Raynier?"

"Yes, milady...mmm, Shahzar?"

Fool, he can't even remember to call me by name as I asked. "Can you read?" she inquired.

"Of course. All in the temple can read."

She frowned. Shahzar went to the bed and slipped past the heavy curtain to stare down at him. He wasn't a boy, and yet he wasn't so old that he appeared ugly. *The silver streaks in his hair are becoming,* she decided. "Can you teach others to read?"

"Yes." His dark eyes bored into her. It softened her anger to look upon him. He was too willing to do what she asked. Shahzar began to wonder if the temple was such a danger to the city and if its usefulness had fully waned. *Maybe Shahmi is wrong to hate the priests, too quick to put an end to something that might be worth saving.*

"I want to ask a favor of you, as your queen." She sidestepped the task at hand, already claiming royal powers though she had none until she'd given birth.

His eyes stayed on hers, waiting for the request. Raynier appeared attentive and loyal. She couldn't be sure though, not yet, not so soon.

"I want you to teach all in the city who desire it, to read and write. I'll give you whatever you require to accomplish this task. My people must have knowledge."

He swallowed. She watched the lump at his throat move slightly. "If that is your wish, Shahzar, I will do as you ask."

"When?"

"In the morning if you wish."

She hadn't expected such obedience. Shahzar sat still, staring back at him with the same boldness he used with her. "You are a handsome man." She pursed her lips, regretting the words as soon as they left her mouth.

Raynier's cheeks flushed in the darkness. "Thank you," he whispered.

Shahzar pulled back the coverlet and climbed in beside him causing him to gasp. "Let us lie here for a while and talk," she said. "I want to know who you are if I'm to have your child." She smiled at her own words. *Yes, that was good. It sounds as if I have a choice in the whole matter.* She'd tried to reason that she did, but the council would stand against her. Although the religion was dying in Kaladia, the traditions held. "Tell me about yourself."

"I was born in Kaladia, on the southern outskirts. My father was a goat herder."

She felt one of his feet swaying back and forth nervously. "Do you remember your father's name?" she pressed. With the exception of her uncle, who had comforted her following her childhood nightmares, Shahzar had never been so close to a man unless they were fighting.

"Yes, I'm his first son; his name was also Raynier."

"And when was the last time you saw your father?"

"When I was seven or eight."

Shahzar shuffled her feet under the covers. The bed felt warm. He was warm. She wanted to touch his hand, just to see what he would do. She reached out to find it, and their fingers intertwined. He breathed deeply then, a priest's trick to try to calm himself. "Do you miss your father?"

"Oh no. The temple is my home. I belong there. I felt the calling of Ishas soon after acceptance into the priesthood. Our Goddess is still present, watching over Kaladia. My service is to our lady, to the faith of Shan-Sei."

She sighed. *He is brainwashed. What to do about him?* Shahzar turned and studied his profile. Thunder crackled nearby. The candlelight was dim at best and within the darkness of the curtains, Raynier had become mostly shadow. "I've decided that you'll teach my people when you return to the temple. But you won't return there tomorrow."

He glanced sideways at her. Shahzar saw a bit of light in his eyes, a reflection from the shard of candlelight that peeked through the opening in the curtain. How she wanted that light to be something more, to be the dark power returned to Kaladia, shining from the eyes of a true Shan-Sei priest. Many a tome procured from Sheah's precious library described the light. Only those trained to see it or proficient in the Gift themselves could notice that light in others. But it was only a reflection, a mirage that faded when he looked away.

"The tradition is that I stay only one night with you. It's forbidden for me to stay longer." Disappointment tainted his words, and his foot went still beneath the coverlet.

"There's no other heir. If I am to be queen, I'll do it in my own way. I'd be a fool to lie with a man I hardly know. I've only just met you; I might not like you at all. If I decide I don't, then I won't have your child, despite your new title. Why would I want the future of my city in the hands of a child sired by an evil man?" She let anger taint her words and his breathing quickened once more. The tradition, the rite and what it entailed, still irked her.

"I'm not evil." His lips pursed together.

"Then stay here longer. The temple teaches patience. You must have such patience." Shahzar lowered her voice. "But I warn you, if you're an evil man, I'll kill you." Her uncle's influence made her say those words.

He drew in a sharp breath, and she felt his dark eyes upon her as if she'd spoken a blasphemous word. "Kill me?"

"You don't believe I can?"

"I...I am a priest," he stammered.

"And I will be queen. I've a dagger under my pillow. I put it there before you came, in case I didn't like you. My uncle has taught me how to kill. Shahmi wants you and all the priests in the temple dead. And he's not the only one."

He swallowed again and his throat made a small clicking sound. Shahzar saw his body go completely still. She'd chilled him with the revelation. *Surely, the priests aren't so sheltered that they don't know the growing hatred for the temple? The commoners don't even understand what the temple is about.* Time and the priests' introverted way of life made them a mystery.

"Are you still in love with me?" she asked in a half whisper, holding back the grin that tried to spread over her lips. Now she would disprove his words. He couldn't possibly care for her now, not after he knew what she was capable of.

"Oh, yes," Raynier answered.

She frowned at his reaction. It made no sense. Thunder raged outside. Shahzar imagined the canals catching the water the sky shed. *At least there will be water. For another year, this rain will give my people life. It might be that long until it rains again.*

She edged closer to him and laid her head against his shoulder. Shahzar took up his other hand trying to calm him. He breathed like an animal caught in a snare, and she wondered if he'd die of fright. She likened his fear to her own. Trapped, in danger, there was nowhere for him to run. For whatever reason, he didn't seem to want to run. "Let us sleep beside each other as friends this night. I like you Raynier. I won't kill you."

-o.O.o-

He nodded, but said nothing. His mind swam with the strange revelations she'd made. Raynier, the new bishop of the failing Shan-Sei temple, had come expecting a rite that would last a few hours, an old tradition symbolizing union between the church and government, a ceremony upheld since the Division. He'd entered Shahzar's chambers completely unaware of the hatred for his kind that lingered in the hearts of the Kaladian people, but he would not leave her room as innocent as when he came.

Chapter Five: The Choice

Shahzar woke to Raynier's voice, a soft melodic chant of sorts as he knelt before the window and sang to the rising sun. At first, she lay still, enjoying the calming effect of his words. Her body was so warm, so at ease. Sleep clung to her mind, tugging her back. Realization slowly set in. She hadn't slept so peacefully since her seventh year. She'd always tossed, turned, risen and grown cold despite the heaviness of the covers when the feeling of the city and all its movements crossed into her dreams.

She slipped through the bed curtains and stood just behind him, wondering if Raynier could feel her there. Not wanting to frighten him, she touched his shoulder. Too many times others had snuck up on her and received the brunt of her quick anger when she turned and struck without question. She doubted he would react the same way, but it didn't hurt to allow him that courtesy.

When he finished his song, he rose and blew out the candle. Shahzar studied his back, the lean muscles beneath his dark skin. She sighed. "You believe."

He nodded. "Shahzar," he paused, weighing his questions. "Why does no one in the castle believe? Where are the icons of Ishas, the talismans about their necks? The shrines?"

Her eyes narrowed in confusion. "What do you mean?"

"Doesn't anyone believe in our Goddess?" he asked.

Shahzar cocked her head to one side, still lost by his meaning. "Shrines? Talismans?" She reached back and grabbed the mass of her loose hair, twisting it into one long rope. The curls had returned overnight, and she hated the wild way they hung around her face.

Raynier held up the charm on his necklace. "Everyone in Kaladia should bear our lady's symbol. Ishas is the city's goddess, yet no one I saw on my way to the castle wore this. There wasn't one shrine." He let the necklace fall back, and Shahzar couldn't help but stare at his bare chest. "Even your bedchamber bears no mark of your faith. How can the queen not have an icon of Ishas?"

"Who said I believe?" She scratched at the nape of her neck and yawned. The priest was certainly brainwashed. Shahzar let go of her hair and frowned when it bounced back into its feral state.

Raynier came forward, that familiar longing in his eyes. She felt it, sensed it and turned away to close the window.

"You asked if I possessed the dark power."

"And you do not." Her hand trembled as she pulled the latch into place. The old window was always hard to shut. "It doesn't mean I believe."

He was behind her when she turned. The closeness startled her, so she sidestepped him and sat down on the bed. As she watched, he lifted the gold chain over his head, an action that made his silver-tinged hair fall against his back. She envied the straightness of it.

"I want you to have this." He came forward in two long steps and bent to place it over her head. It brought him close. She couldn't help but close her eyes and breathe in the scent of him, smokewood incense and something else familiar, like spring flowers.

As he moved to sit beside her, Shahzar touched the intricate talisman. She'd seen renderings of Ishas in books, but never held one. A wave of emotion swept over her. She'd felt it before, that strange, cold feeling of connection to some other thing.

"What's wrong?" Raynier's voice sounded so very far away.

The city moved and it was day. Shahzar wasn't in the throes of a nightmare, but her mind traced the outer walls and then the second walls which were more ancient and touched by time. The vision spiraled around Kaladia until finally, it centered on the Shan-Sei temple and that being beneath the earth, that force she couldn't understand.

"Shahzar?" Raynier asked.

She cringed when he touched her shoulder. The talisman fell away until the connection dropped and the coppery trinket bumped against the gauze dress she wore, severing the strange vision from her mind. "If you believe then all hope is not lost." She hadn't expected those words to come out, but she said them nonetheless. Her icy gaze softened. She felt entranced by his faith, the very thing that would guarantee the temple's future.

There was a soft knock on the door.

"Come in, Inell," Shahzar called impatiently, her stone-cold look returning. She moved away from the bishop and went to her desk. There she stood, nervously twisting a lock of her black hair around her fingers.

The carved door opened, and the wide-eyed servant entered the room. She stared at Raynier as though he were a strange thing. Even as she spoke to Shahzar, she wouldn't take her eyes from him. "Milady, your uncle has called a council meeting. He's requested your presence. He sent me to see if you needed help…" she hesitated, "…with the priest."

Smiling brilliantly, Shahzar leaned toward the girl and touched her shoulder as if in friendship. A bitter laugh echoed in her words when she spoke. "Tell my uncle that the priest is alive and well, and I'll keep him so until it suits me to do otherwise. I will attend the council meeting as soon as I'm properly dressed."

"Yes, milady." The servant left the room with a backward glance. Shahzar could sense the hatred in Inell's eyes, but was uncertain why the woman would suddenly feel that way. It could only mean her uncle had shared the plot. Shahmi was clever at persuasion.

"Shall I go back to the temple?" Raynier asked. He fingered the edge of his robes where they lay across the bedside table. His expression was one of half-hidden yearning, a desire to stay.

She turned on him, still smiling. "Oh, no. If you go to the temple now, Shahmi will kill you on your way out." She went back to him and stood close enough to brush her fingers over the hairs on his chest, making his breathing stumble. "It's best you stay here in my room. You're safe here."

Raynier slumped on the bed in shock over Shahzar's comment.

"When I'm at the meeting, you can bathe. Inell will bring you fresh robes." She reached up and pushed his hair away from his face. "You will wear your hair uncovered when you're here. I prefer it that way."

Time stopped as he stared into her eyes. *What am I doing?* she wondered. She knew she shouldn't be playing such games. Her uncle would be angry. This was the first time she'd disobeyed him.

Inell knocked at the door again and entered. She cringed even before she spoke. "Your uncle is unhappy; you must meet with him at once."

Shahzar knew Inell's tone. The little servant expected a reprimand. She narrowed her dark eyes as if daring her to offer more foul news.

"Help me to dress, Inell." She entered the bathing room with the frightened, woman. When she returned, finely dressed in a stifling red gown, hair plaited and veiled, she found Raynier sitting on the bed in the same place as she'd left him. His face was pale as though he'd seen a ghost. Her pillow was askew and she guessed he'd found the dagger hidden there.

"Don't leave this room," Shahzar whispered. She reached over and touched his shoulder. "Remember, you're safe here. After Inell brings you fresh robes, bar the door. Let no one in but me."

Raynier nodded, his face lined with worry.

When Shahzar turned to leave, her eyes had gone cold, her lips drawing down in an angry way. It was the mask she wore, a cold, unyielding countenance. "I'm ready," she said to Inell. She had no intention of speaking with Shahmi before the meeting.

-o.O.o-

She swept into the council room and took her seat beneath the tapestry that depicted two griffons and a crown. Shahzar crossed her hands in her lap and watched Horlan and Rond file in. The others were already gathered. Shahmi had a pained look in his eyes and he stared at her, pleading without words for some explanation.

Sheah rapped her stick against the table and called the meeting to order. "You summoned us all, Shahmi," the speaker began, turning her oval-shaped face toward the captain. "What is of such urgency?"

Shahzar saw the flash of anger in her uncle's eyes before he nodded at Sheah. Shahmi ran his hand over his cropped hair and took a deep breath. The princess knew what was supposed to happen. They'd rehearsed it all, down to the last detail. The bishop was supposed to be dead. Inell was supposed to have come in on the scene and the council was to give the death sentence for the rest of the priesthood. Now, all that was implausible.

"With the increasing raids, I beseech the council to reinforce the outer and secondary walls. I know many of you think this is a frivolous request and that it could wait for the scheduled meeting, but I..." Shahmi's voice faltered and Shahzar felt responsible.

"I second this motion," she said, standing.

She'd been to the meetings since leaving the foot soldiers, but this was the first time the princess had spoken. All the council turned toward her. Shahzar looked the part, her face stoic, her crimson-colored clothing matching the traditional veiled and hidden requirements of her station.

Antirion stood. Shahzar bit her bottom lip, betraying her nerves. She watched the mason beneath half-lowered eyelids. He was rough-looking, thick on the top with worn hands and ebony skin from days spent working under the sunlight. Yet, he wore the bright yellow Kyannel sash that symbolized his rank among the guilds. The silky fabric contradicted Antirion's appearance, but his smooth voice and long drawn speech made up for it. He stood behind the motion, backing Shahmi and Shahzar. The princess knew his reasons. Building the new walls would increase his future wages and make him a richer man.

When the meeting adjourned, Shahzar filed out with the rest of the members. She felt Shahmi shadowing her, waiting for the right moment for the eventual confrontation. It came as she passed the guards at the last arch in the hall. She was almost safe, almost back to her room.

"Why isn't he dead?"

Shahzar stopped at the foot of the marble stairs and looked over her shoulder. Her uncle's mouth was a tight line, his eyes reflecting the anger over her disobedience. Shahmi had one hand on the hilt of his scimitar and that alone made her turn fully.

"The temple is under my protection now." She was sweating from the meeting and the trek back to her room. The damnable dress was too heavy for the heat of day, even with the windows draped and the thick brick and plaster walls of the castle.

"I won't leave here. I'll wait until he comes down." He tapped the hilt of his blade with meaning.

Shahzar understood. She also knew there was no sense in arguing with her uncle when he was angry. She held onto the banister and raced up the stairs, half expecting him to follow. She rapped at the door. "It's me, Shahzar." She looked down to see Shahmi still waiting. No one came to answer or unbar the door. Shahzar pulled the handle, and her stomach twisted when it opened. He hadn't listened, hadn't done what she said. "Raynier, you fool." She sighed and crossed the threshold, barring the door herself.

Raynier was as she'd left him, unbathed and still dressed in only his black pants. He sat on the edge of the bed. The bundle of clothing Inell had brought him was there beside his pillow. He had hardly touched the tray of food, which sat at the bedside.

Wringing her hands together, she stalked past Raynier. Shahzar stopped at the window and growled in frustration. "Why didn't you bathe?"

"I must return to the temple now."

Shahzar attempted to untie her dress bindings. She struggled with them, defeated. The princess rushed to the bed and sought her dagger. When she pulled it out, Raynier gasped.

For a moment she only looked at him, puzzled. Then she drew the blade from its sheath and slashed the bindings at her waist, sides and wrists. The outer shell of the red dress fell to the carpet in a soft, crumpled pile of heavy fabric. His eyes widened. The chemise she wore was moist from sweat. It clung to her body in a way that made his face burn.

She scoffed, angry at the world. "Oh, the things I'll change when I'm queen." Shahzar slid the dagger back into its sheath and carelessly tossed it onto the desk. It crashed and became lost among the scrolls. She clasped her hands in front of her chest and closed her eyes, trying to regain her calm. "Must you go now?"

"I feel I should. I'm unsuitable for the post of bishop. The temple will send another priest to you."

"Hm." One brow rose when she looked at him. Sincerity flowed in her voice. "I don't want another priest." Unhappy with his words, she went into the bathing room and turned on the water. It took less time for the pressure to build from the heated reservoir beneath the building because of the recent rains. A thin veil of steam rose in the air. It followed after Shahzar when she came to fetch him.

"I forbid you to go." Her voice was bitter. "Shahmi followed me to my room. He's waiting at the steps to kill you." When his face didn't change, she went on. "Don't you understand?"

He pursed his lips and shook his head. "Please, I want to go back to the temple. Life makes no sense here. If your uncle wanted me dead, he could have done it when he brought me to your room yesterday."

"Go and see for yourself if you don't believe me."

Raynier sighed and turned to go. He unbarred the door, opened it and walked out. The princess followed, retrieving her dagger once more. The bishop peered down the long rows of marble steps. At the landing, the captain of the guards stared up at him.

Shahmi's boots clicked as he began his slow ascent. Raynier tightened his grip on the banister, frozen in place. Shahmi's hand was still on the handle of his sword. He looked like an angry father coming to avenge his daughter's honor.

Behind the bishop, a blade whispered. Shahzar had drawn her dagger. She took Raynier's hand. Their fingers intertwined as they had the night before. Her uncle stopped, catching the movement. His brows became a crooked V above his stark eyes.

"Step down, Shahmi. Only a queen can rule, and I'm the last in the Galkwin line." Her voice held true malice in it. She squeezed Raynier's hand. "No harm will come to you if you stay with me," she murmured.

"The temple serves itself. It won't serve you, Shahzar. Give him to me since you don't have the courage to do it yourself," Shahmi demanded.

"It takes no courage to murder!"

"It will be easier without them. You know it's the right thing to do. We've been over this." He took another step, focused on her figure, ready for the slightest sign of movement.

"You want revenge for your sister. Your hatred blinds you." It stung him. She'd said it for that purpose alone. Worse yet, she knew it was true.

Shahzar realized why her uncle wanted the temple gone. "You blame the Shan-Sei for her death."

"Ridiculous," he spat. "You foolish girl. This man cares nothing for you." He took another step. She remained still. The priest at her side stood frozen with fear. "It will take only a moment to kill him." He started up faster, determined to see the end of his plan.

Her fingers tensed, her mind set. In a flash, Shahzar left Raynier's side. She caught Shahmi with the force of her lithe body. Uncle and niece rolled down the stairs in a violent struggle for control. When they reached the landing, she pinned Shahmi down. She held the blade to his throat, the same dagger he'd given her as a gift long ago. In the dim light cast from the shrouded windows, she saw a trickle of his blood against the white marble.

Shahmi didn't struggle. He was no match for her. His features said it all. In the long, drawn silence that followed, she asserted her will, her dominance. "If you cross over these steps again, I'll kill you. If you harm this man, I'll kill you. I'm the queen. Do not forget that!"

After a time, she let him rise. He eyed her as she spoke, wary of her anger. "You deserve the name I gave you at birth. You are a warrior. Even now, though you go against my wishes, you don't shame me. I'll be proud to call you my queen when that day comes." He lowered his eyes. It was a look she knew, a submissive gesture of fear, one she'd never wanted to witness in her uncle. He turned and left, his boots clicking against the stone floor.

Shahzar watched him go, no longer the unstoppable hero she imagined he was. Her guilt twisted into anger. It wasn't supposed to be this way. She turned her attention to Raynier. "I told you." The princess marched back up the steps and grasped his arm to tug him into the safety of her room. She barred the door and once more threw her dagger. It hit the wall above her desk and clattered among the onyx sleeves.

"I forbid you to leave," she said under her breath, giving Raynier a scathing look. He nodded and sat back on the edge of the bed. Shahzar stomped into the bathing room.

She sank into the water and closed her eyes. "I shouldn't have done this," she muttered. "I can't...that shouldn't have happened..." Shahzar pursed her lips. Her fists clenched beneath the bathwater and she let her body slide under. The princess held her breath, so startled over her rebellion that she didn't know what to do next. She enjoyed the protective feeling of the water covering her. She stayed there until she couldn't stand it any longer. She came up and washed her hair, determined to calm down. It wasn't the same as having Inell do it for her, but it would have to do.

"Raynier!" she called when she finished, her voice still heavy with anger and frustration. She dried off and slung a dressing gown over her body.

"Yes?" he called from the bedroom.

"Come in here with me."

He entered the bathing room, the veil of steam surrounding him in wisps of gray. His bare feet were dark against the green, stone floor. Shahzar watched him from the gilt chair beside the massive tub. Her hair hung loose in wild curls, still damp and warm against her back. "Strip and get into the bath. I want to wash your hair."

He nodded, a look of fear tightening his face. The bishop pushed down his pants and glanced at her. She looked away, into the water. When Raynier positioned himself inside the tub, she poured warm water over his body and massaged soap into his scalp. Shahzar took on the duties Inell had done countless times to her in an attempt to soothe her nerves. She remained silent, engrossed in the task at hand. Once satisfied, she poured water over him again. Bubbles eddied around his body in swirls. His back was to her.

Still with no clue why she decided to let him live, she got up and rubbed her temples. "Dry yourself. It's late."

Raynier turned in time to see her walking away.

When he finally came back to the bedroom, he was clothed only in a thick, white towel. Inell had come with the day's scrolls. The servant gasped and looked down while Raynier went to fetch a pair of clean pants from the pile on the bed that she left earlier.

Shahzar sat at her desk, unfurling scroll after scroll. She read aloud, her voice dull as she scanned tallies and meeting minutes. She dropped another sleeve onto her desk and unrolled the paper it guarded. She waved Inell away with an absent flick of her wrist. "I'm tired. Leave me."

The servant slipped out without a word. The door clicked shut and Shahzar looked at it, wondering if she should bar it again. The image of her defeated uncle haunted her, and she shook her head. "Raynier, please get into my bed and warm the covers. The day has been long. I'm tired and want nothing more than to sleep in your arms."

She blew out the candles in the room. It was black as pitch when she slid into the bed beside him. Shahzar put her arms around his waist and savored his warmth. Resting her head against his chest as she'd done the night before, she listened to the beating of his heart slow.

After a long while, he touched her face with his fingertips. He traced her lips and cheeks in slow gentle strokes. When she sighed, he jumped.

"Forgive me," he whispered. "Did I wake you?"

"No," she replied softly. For the first time, Shahzar wondered what it would be like to be so close to someone and not have him fear her. She regretted disobeying her uncle, but not her reasoning for it. Raynier no more deserved death than her mother had. And she guessed the other priests in the Shan-Sei temple were the same. "Why you?" she asked.

"What do you mean?"

"Of the three candidates Toman had to choose from, why did he pick you?"

Raynier swallowed hard. "Toman said he chose me for my faith in Ishas."

She held him tighter, her dark eyes focusing on the sliver of dim light past the bed curtains. *Faith. Toman had chosen him on that. It seems the only strength Raynier has,* she thought. He wasn't strong-willed or even persuasive, but he believed in the Goddess. She closed her eyes and rubbed her cheek against the soft hairs on his chest. She reached for the shape of Ishas, the small talisman he'd given her. Her fingers ran along each curve. The sweeping vision didn't come to her again, but she did feel a connection to an old entity longing for release.

Chapter Six: Sleepless

Raynier retreated from the bed at his usual early hour. He didn't want to leave her side, the warmth or the sweet scent of lavender and fig that perfumed Shahzar's skin. But it was time to sing the morning prayers. Not a day passed since his induction into the temple that he hadn't done so. He opened the arched window, marveling for an instant at the stained glass. The bishop found the stub of a pale taper, its end not quite burned down to nothing. He lit it and knelt, making the sign of the holy circle above his head before he started to sing.

He heard her yawn halfway through the melody. Raynier wanted to turn, hoped that when he did she'd be watching him with her melting eyes. He resisted. The remainder of the prayer sounded rushed, but he doubted she would notice. Nothing in her room indicated her faith in Ishas, although he felt she did believe. He blew out the candle and turned at last.

"How can you be in love with me?" Shahzar asked, her voice still slurred from sleep. Her eyes drooped and she appeared comfortable on the bed, one hand holding back the bed curtains.

Raynier looked down at her, his chest heavy with a longing desire to climb back into that warmth with her. Her question wasn't something he could fully answer. He didn't speak for a little while, formulating the answer.

"Well?" she prodded, one brow rising.

He took a deep breath and tried to explain it. "You're beautiful," he blurted, but that didn't feel substantial enough so he went on. "You hold yourself with such dignity and you're fearless. At first, I thought I'd go mad if I didn't see you again. And then, when Toman said I was his choice as bishop, I thought I'd go mad when I did. I was afraid after the rite that I'd be lost from you forever."

"Is that how it will be? Will you be lost from me?" Shahzar stretched her arms high. She yawned again, her gilt eyes returning to his face.

"That's the way it's supposed to be," he said, though he didn't want it to end.

"Mmm." She twisted off the bed and walked to her desk, wriggling her toes in the thick green carpet. Shahzar pushed aside a bundle of scrolls and sought out the ones she wanted.

Raynier followed her, unsure of himself. He stood just behind her side, not willing to move closer. His gaze swept across the desk and he saw a few words that blazed on the parchment she studied. "Al-Shing?" he asked, reading the familiar name.

Shahzar let go of the scroll. The parchment curled in on itself, hiding her secrets. She spun around to face him, causing Raynier to take a step back.

Her eyes reflected the light like a lion's, all golden and predatory. "Are you spying on me?"

"I'm sorry," he replied, his voice too soft to be anything but honest. "I didn't mean to invade your privacy." Her reaction startled him. Shahzar seemed so angry, so wild and unapproachable, yet she'd held him all through the night. She was a contradiction in every way.

Her eyes narrowed on him, but she said nothing more. He could feel her gaze lowering across his chest. She twisted a lock of her hair around her forefinger.

"The ways of the priesthood are there to protect us all," Raynier said. "The Shan-Sei and the royal family cannot grow too close. It's dangerous. But what I said to you last night..." His mouth hung open as he struggled for the words. "About how I feel..."

She shook her head, her smirk twisting. "I'm to have your child. Is there any closer arrangement than that?" She flicked away a tendril of her hair and turned back to her papers.

"The dark power is forbidden with good reason." That scroll bore the name of the old Shan-Sei priest. Al-Shing had been one of the priests responsible for the wastelands. Shahzar pushed the scroll into a high pile where it became lost. *She's hiding it from me,* Raynier thought.

"The temple has brainwashed you to believe in its ways without question." She turned to face him.

"That's not true," he replied, clenching his fists.

"Who do the Shan-Sei serve?"

"We serve the creator, Ishas." He couldn't believe she'd even asked the question. Everyone ought to know the purpose of the Shan-Sei.

Moreover, all those in the castle should be venerating the patron Goddess of their city.

"And what good is that? I ask you because the council will ask it. I don't think you realize how much danger your precious temple is in." Her temper quickened. It crinkled the space between her black eyebrows and tightened her mouth.

Raynier shook his head. "My priests want nothing but peace, to serve Ishas. It's our calling."

Shahzar's lips pursed just before she came at him. Raynier flinched, but held his ground. She caught his shoulders and almost shook him, but the anger in her eyes suddenly vanished. "The Shan-Sei should serve more! Your priests live because of the protection my guards give this city. They live off the tithe of food and supplies its people send you each month. They live because a few still believe in the dark power, which you say no longer exists there! A thing you try to warn me of!"

"I warn you because I see your hunger for it!" he shouted. Shahzar's desire for the old ways worried him. He knew he had to stop her and find a way to make her understand the true grace of Ishas. Shahzar stood close to him, too near to be ignored. Raynier let his hands find purchase on her narrow waist. "The priests that held that power left and with good reason." He tried to pull her closer, but she shrugged away from his touch.

"Why? Tell me why it's so wrong!"

Raynier let his hands fall to his sides, disappointed that she'd moved away. Shahzar looked angry and ready to fight him. "You have only to look at the wastelands. There you have the answer," he said in a gentler tone.

"Then why should I let you live? Why should the council suffer your priests to exist? You warn me of the dark power, and yet you tell me I should have icons of Ishas in my room. It doesn't make sense." She shook her head and pointed at him. "You don't realize how close you are to the edge of death. The council members don't care if the guards raze the temple to the ground. The people fear you, all of you, cloistered away behind your sacred walls. Once, only the Klemish hated the Shan-Sei, but no one knows what the temple represents anymore, and now your own people are growing to hate you."

"The Shan-Sei represent Ishas. Nothing has changed. We've always been that. We serve the Goddess; we worship her."

"That's what you'll tell the council and the guards when they come to burn the temple down? No! It's not enough. They know nothing of your goddess. Ishas is a shadow whispered about in fairy tales. When they ask you, you'll say the priests serve the Goddess and all the people of Kaladia. And you'll need to change the ways of your temple. Make the council believe the answer I've just supplied you. If you don't, then I'll not stay them any longer. The council and the guard will burn it to the ground and every last priest will be put to death. I can't hold Shahmi back forever." She crossed her arms, her eyes feral.

Raynier couldn't breathe. She'd shocked him. "I don't understand…" he began. How could there be so much hatred? The Shan-Sei in the temple were innocent, forced to live in the wake of the old ones' terrible legacy.

Shahzar stalked toward him and grabbed his wrist. She guided him to her desk to sit. "Let me show you." She hissed. "I want you to understand!" The princess pushed the scrolls and sealed sleeves to one side, clearing a workspace for him. She counted as she rifled through another pile of meeting minutes, nodded and then dropped three scrolls in front of him.

Raynier's dark eyes caught the council's words, on the lines of prejudice and hatred so blatantly listed there. "…And it is our opinion that the temple stands in the way of progress. Its tithes, though not draining, are a support the Kaladians shouldn't feel obligated to pay. There is no return on the bargain, no goods or services rendered for the food provided..." he read aloud.

"And this one." She growled. "Look here." She unfurled another and weighted it with two sleeves. She jabbed a finger at the passage.

"This is the reason the Klemish keep raiding our city, because they hate the Shan-Sei. We are no longer Shan-Sei. We are Kaladian. In time, this council will have to purge the city of the blemish, the symbol of the old ways. We can't take the raids for these few priests and..."

"You see?" Shahzar asked.

Raynier tentatively reached for another, so as not to anger her. "Can I read them all?"

"I think you should. Take all day if you like." She went to get the chair from beside the door, dragging it across the carpet to his side. When she seated herself, her anger visibly dissipated. "It's not acceptable for you to be so sheltered," she said in a tender voice. "If the temple is to survive then it must become a player in the government or at least hold sway over the people." She reached in front of him and snatched up another sleeve. Together the two huddled over her desk for hours on end until he finally digested the information and the fact that the people had forgotten Ishas.

When night came, Raynier pushed the papers away and bent his head, clutching his temples in both hands. "That's enough," he whispered. "I don't know what to do. Everything is against me, the council, the people, your uncle." For years, the hatred had spread like unchecked weeds in the hearts of those outside the temple. Just understanding the blind prejudice frustrated Raynier.

Shahzar placed one hand on his shoulder. "Now you know. We can save it, all of it—the temple, the priests and the faith." She smiled at him and stood. "Come. Let me wash your hair. It will help you relax and allow you time to think."

Raynier let her lead him to the bath. He watched her draw the water and sprinkle salts within. At once, the gray steam drifted from the heated water. He turned away from her and pulled off his clothes, too shy to meet her gaze. The bishop stepped into the bath and hurried to sit down.

Behind him, Shahzar dipped a clay bowl into the water and drew it out. "Close your eyes," she murmured. She poured the calming, heated water over him. The princess rubbed soap into his hair, humming under her breath so softly that he could barely make out the familiar tune. She rinsed the soap away and leaned forward to massage his temples. The weight of all he'd studied spun within his thoughts. Raynier slowed his breathing, and tried to think of a solution. Shahzar's voice drifted around him, and the feel of her fingers caressing his skin helped ease his worries.

"I need to lie down," he said when she stopped. He turned and caught her fingers before she could pull them away. "You can't keep me in your bedchamber forever. I'll have to go back. I have to face this." He ran his thumb over the back of her hand, hoping she'd return his affections.

"You'll have my protection." Shahzar lowered her eyes and pulled her hand away. "I served under my uncle in the foot-soldiers. The council is already starting to fear me, as they should." She glanced up again, an unapproachable look in her eyes, one he'd seen before. "Dry yourself. Let me have some time in the bath to think. Go rest and I will join you soon." Shahzar held the towel for him when he stood. She focused on the wall, apparently unwilling to see him without his body covered.

-o.O.o-

Much later, Shahzar joined him in the bed, sighing at the comfort of his warmth. She moved nearer to Raynier. *Am I letting myself get too close? Are you a danger to me?* she wondered. "As you know, there was a plot against your life. It was my uncle's idea that I kill you in my bed, claiming you were trying to strangle me. It would have been an excuse to wipe out the temple. It would have worked, but I ruined that for him."

"Why did you spare me?" He reached for her hand and clasped it tight.

Shahzar shifted her feet and their legs touched beneath the blanket. She tried to free her hand, but gave up too easily. Instead, she pressed her cheek against his shoulder and closed her eyes. *Because you said you loved me,* she thought, but she couldn't tell him that. Shahmi's warnings about love and growing too attached to anyone haunted her. "You did nothing wrong, nothing to deserve Shahmi's hatred."

"That's the only reason?" he asked.

She felt his cheek press against the top of her head and for a second she wondered what it would be like to look up, to kiss him. "I think it's reason enough." She sighed and pushed her other arm beneath him, tugging his body closer.

"Do you believe in Ishas, in the ways of the Shan-Sei?" he whispered.

"I will never lie to you," she said. "I do believe in Ishas. I believe in the Shan-Sei. I'm trying to save the temple, for I hope against hope that the true priests will return to us. The dark power saved this city from the Klemish. It sent them away. I know it made the wastelands, but maybe it could bring things back, change it to what it once was."

"I don't have the dark power," Raynier declared. "My father sent me to the priests to give me a better life. Every one of the priests will tell you a similar story." He caressed her hand with his thumb, a slow, gentle touch.

"I know that," Shahzar said, tension quavering in her voice.

His fingers moved over her arm, rested on her shoulder for a moment, and then he cupped her cheek tenderly. "But, Shahzar, have you thought of yourself?"

"What do you mean?" His warm hand glided over her face. She felt torn between her instinct to pull away and her desire to remain close to him.

"Have you not seen the light in your own eyes?"

"What are you saying?" She tilted her head up, squinting at his dark face melded with the shadows.

"You're a Galkwin. The Shan-Sei sired some part of you, the true priests with the dark power. I swear I saw that light reflected in your eyes when you crossed the courtyard in the temple, when you looked at me through the glass. And again in the circle room when you met with Toman. It's small, but I've read enough to know what it looks like."

The princess was silent. *Can this be? Can I have some part of the magic in me? Is it possible that I'm searching in vain for something I may already have?* The notion piqued her curiosity, made possibilities rise she hadn't considered.

"Shahzar?"

"Be silent. You tire me with your strange words. Hold me close; I feel so cold tonight." With that, she curled against him and let him comb his fingers slowly through her hair. She closed her eyes, feigning sleep. He traced her lips with his forefinger in slow, fluid movements. It tickled in a faint way. After a time, he traced her chin and then her neck until, at last, he put his hand over her side and held her.

When Raynier's breathing steadied and his hand felt heavy across her body, she climbed out of bed. Shahzar padded across the rug and took the candle from the windowsill. She looked over her shoulder to be sure Raynier hadn't stirred. The bed-curtains remained flaccid. Satisfied, she crept into the bathing room. The princess pulled out a chair and sat down in front of the polished, metal mirror, lighting a candle from a smaller one that burned on the shelf nearby. Shahzar leaned forward and studied the flecks of gold in her dark, brown eyes. She waited, keeping her eyelids as wide as she could, watching for what Raynier claimed to see. The candlelight flickered in the black of her pupils, but she saw nothing mysterious there. *It cannot be true. It's not.*

She stood and blew out the candle. Her body involuntarily shook before it calmed. Her hair was still damp from the bath, so she blamed that and her thin sleeping gown for the chill. Another wave of cold struck her in the arched entry before she passed back to the bedchamber. Shahzar rubbed her upper arms with her hands to ward the sensation away. She hurried to the bed and climbed under the warm coverlet, moving back beside Raynier. Carefully, she replaced his arm over her side. He muttered in his sleep and reflexively latched onto her body, tugging her to his chest.

A chill came again. She shivered against Raynier and tried to go to sleep. The dream began as it usually did, along the outer wall of Kaladia. Only this time it strayed further. Her mind carried her vision around the perimeter of the city, washing over herds of sheep and goats. The animals were still, sleeping in huddled heaps. The wasteland sand glowed blue in the joined moonlight.

Shahzar rolled in her sleep so that her back pressed into Raynier's chest. The chills became more intense, as did the voices and the movements in the shadows of the dunes. She tried not to hear, tried to look away, her mind seeking that safe place in the Shan-Sei temple, that surge of energy beneath the circle room, but the vision wouldn't let her guide the nightmare. It forced her back, drew her to the moving shadows. They emerged from the dunes in a charging line. The riders breached the gates, and she could hear a shepherd screaming. The nightmare showed her the suffering man, his long, pale tunic coated with blood.

Shahzar's eyes opened wide. Her body shot up of its own accord, her mind trailing groggily behind. Her fingers felt numb and icy. Her legs, buried deep within the coverlet and intertwined with Raynier's, seemed even colder.

"No, no, no," she rasped. "Not now, not this night." A desperate wave of agony swept over her. Again, she left the bed. This time she pulled on her gold-colored robe and tied the belt before she left her room. Shahzar raced down the marble steps, her wild, black hair flying behind her. She sprinted through the empty, arched halls. Her bare feet thumped on the tiles, the sound echoing in the stillness. The princess knew her way even in the dark. She'd come to this chamber countless times, even before the nightmares and the cold. She turned the handle and rushed into Shahmi's room, a wave of guilt stabbing at her for betraying him. Shahzar caught her breath and stopped beside his bed. He was a stony shape in the darkness. Shahmi woke easily, as always, when she placed her hand on his forehead.

"Are they coming?" he whispered. Though he was sound asleep only a moment before, her familiar touch alerted him to the danger. It was a secret they shared, the cold she felt when the raiders came.

"Worse, Shahmi." Her voice caught in her throat. This hadn't happened before. "They're in the city."

He rose and pulled on his padded tunic. Shahmi threw on his belt, the weapons thudding against each other. Shahzar stood there, the painting of her mother glaring down on her, making her feel responsible for what had happened. Since her seventh year, she'd always known when the raiders were coming or when they were near. That night, they'd come and she hadn't felt it. The heat of Raynier's body so close to hers had dulled the sensations and let her sleep until the people cried out and her curse could not be ignored.

"I should've killed him," she muttered to herself. The cold struck again. She shuddered and felt the vision sweeping into focus. "They're just past the second wall, at the southern gate!"

Shahmi nodded, his face stern. "The cold will be gone soon, Shahzar." He took a step toward her, touched her shoulder and frowned. "Don't let it take you too far. I'll stop them. I always do."

"Ishas, please…" she began, but her uncle turned just before he left and gave her an icy look. The princess sat down on his bed and silenced her voice. Prayer was not something Shahmi trusted. He ran his hand over his shorn hair and stalked out to gather his troops. Shahzar was never wrong about the raiders. It was a gift her mother had grown into before she died, a gift Shahmi trusted much more than prayers to a goddess that had long since abandoned the city. He'd told Shahzar about the curse the first night she came running to his room, shivering with the cold and drained by the nightmares of raiders.

Shahzar waited until the warning bells clanged out in the night. Shahmi would stop them, kill them or at least drive them back into the desert. She clutched the charm Raynier had given her and began again. It was the first time she prayed to Ishas. She reached out with her mind, calling on the goddess to wake from her long slumber and protect Kaladia once more. The vision shifted at last, drawing her mind to the circle room where she'd first met Raynier. She succumbed to dizziness and fell back against the mattress. The cold enveloped her, and she could feel the touch of Ishas.

The goddess spoke in a shifting, shadowy voice: "No one hears me but you..."

Chapter Seven: Night Terror

The Klemish army infiltrated Kaladia with the help of the mercenaries now in its ranks. Most were stealthy assassins, trained in the outer wasteland city of Bisura. Riel watched as they lurked in the shadows, working in unison to mark and shoot down the archers on watch atop the high wall. That they could do so soundlessly, felling their targets without drawing attention, made him wonder what other capabilities the men possessed. The mercenaries held talents beyond the scope of the captain's own men. He wondered if their blood was tainted by Gifts not unlike the dark power from the days of old.

Riel girded his camel, crying out for the monster of a beast to keep up with Tustin's as the army passed the gates. Dalin broke away, chasing the men filtering down a city street. *He wants to taste the blood*, Riel thought. *Always wants to be in the thick of death*. The captain felt no desire to get so close. Duty dictated that he protect his king.

He tugged his camel's head to the right when Tustin turned. The king and his guards trampled through a smaller street, seeking out the temple of Shan-Sei. None of the men knew the way for sure, but they'd studied the old maps and read the histories of their mother city. Past the first wall and the second, the landmarks changed in time with those generation-old descriptions.

Something about Kaladia troubled Riel. The White City looked too much like Klem. True, the plastered-covered stones that made up her walls contrasted with Klem's shadowy black ones, but the night all but hid the difference. The layout of the arched entries to the merchant strip, the curved architecture and even the old symbols burned into the front doors of people's homes — all these things rang with familiarity.

Tustin, his face shrouded in azure fabric and his head guarded by a helm that glowed in the triple moonlight, slowed his mount and glanced at him. The men stood at a series of streets, all forking away in different directions. "Which way, Captain?" the king called.

Riel studied their surroundings. According to legend, all Kaladian streets led to the temple; all homes bore at least one window that faced the holy building. The clues should be easy to decipher and yet, as he squinted at the homes they passed, he saw no evidence of that myth. He looked up, past the shadowy laundry strung between two high windows and flapping in the night breeze. A single, pale minaret rose beyond the row of plaster-walled homes. Riel raised a gloved hand, his eyes catching on the shadows in the open, arched window of one house. A woman, her straight, black hair hanging loose, her face aghast with horror, stood in that open window holding a lit oil lamp. She watched the men.

Euphenia, Riel thought. He knew it couldn't be his wife, that his prize of a well-cared for woman rested safe in her bed far across the desert. The resemblance tore at him nevertheless. The wind picked up and tendrils of the watcher's hair drifted across her face. Euphenia looked just like that before she went to bed. She sat at the window that overlooked the royal gardens, brushing the braids from her hair and taking in the scent of lilies her husband had traded for when they first moved there.

"This way, my king," he said. "I see one of the four minarets just there." He pointed past the window, hoping the king would take no notice of the woman. He prayed to Daumion that the watcher would turn and disappear into the shadows of her home.

A sickening wail broke out over the city. Riel knew, not two streets over, that the massacre began. Tustin's army of mercenaries mingled with Klemish soldiers loyal to the king, cut down people, killing anyone unfortunate enough to be out on the streets. Riel knew they were innocent, as free of corruption as any of the merchants and families back home. Their untimely deaths came because of a ruthless king blinded by old hatred. *I follow a madman*, he decided. With sudden ardor, Riel silently prayed to his god for forgiveness.

The king and his entourage of high guards moved away from the homes, away from the haunting watcher. The stars that twinkled above were the same as those back home. The night air even smelled of the same soap Klemish dwellers used to wash their linens. Riel thought he would die from guilt. "These are not my people," he reminded himself aloud. "Not mine, not the people of Klem." He didn't harbor the same hatred that seethed inside Tustin. The captain felt no passion for war, or vengeance over his people's exile. The pain of it happened before his time, and Kaladia could never replace the city he lived in. "This conquest is absurd," Riel muttered. Fortunately, the other guards didn't hear his voice through the blue-black fabric that swathed his mouth.

Screams of terror continued to echo in the darkness. The first and second moons were close to their nightly union with the third. Riel came to Tustin's side. The captain cringed when he heard Dalin's blood-curling war cry. The king chuckled. His brother only howled like that when he'd killed someone.

"Ah, I see it," Tustin said. Riel noticed the sparkle in his king's black eyes. "Tonight we slaughter the Shan-Sei. Let them pay for what they did to us."

Suddenly, bells clanged out over the screams. The disruptive bonging echoed and grew as more bells sounded on the first wall. Riel looked back, then to the either side, panic seizing his heart. *If they kill him, I will run,* he realized with certainty. *Euphenia will not know days without me at her side.*

Tustin let out a garbled growl of disgust. He slapped his mount's rump, sending the war camel galloping forward rather than back the way they'd come. Riel clenched the reins and wondered if this would be it; if this night he'd be free of the king's madness. He hoped so. Duty bade him to move forward and he did, clinging to his saddle, ready to retreat when the Kaladian guards challenged them. *It must look like I tried to defend him.*

The Klemish captain didn't have long to wait. Kaladian foot soldiers poured from the wide, brick street ahead. Squat, plastered homes sat on either side, leaving no path for retreat between. "My king!" Riel shouted, charging to Tustin's side.

The Klemish leader didn't turn. His gaze remained fixed on the bulbous dome and four minarets that rose above the buildings in front of him. Foot soldiers ran full-speed and, for a moment, Riel thought the end had come at last. The king's guards plowed forward, their war camels crushing the mount-less soldiers underfoot.

"There are too many!" Riel shouted. "My king! Tustin!" He leaned forward, his hand grasping the king's reins. Without another thought, he sealed his future and pulled Tustin's mount away. He looped the reins over his saddle and girded his camel into retreat. The two men's camels raced over the cobbles. One man longed for life and the other desired ruin.

"We were so close," Tustin cried out. "Riel!"

The captain didn't stop. He didn't want to turn. He knew his king, and he understood the punishment he deserved for what he just did. Retreat represented cowardice. Tustin's anger awaited him in the tents beyond the dunes, but Riel didn't care. He trembled when he heard the swishing sound of Tustin's blade escaping its sheath. *Not now*, Riel pleaded with his god. *Don't let him take me, Daumion. I beg you.*

Instead of the blow he expected, Riel felt the reins he'd purloined slacken. "Coward!" Tustin raged as his scimitar whizzed past Riel's ear. His mount now freed from the captain's, the king broke away, charging for the same street Dalin disappeared down earlier.

Riel pulled back on his reins. His mount turned in a circle, giving the captain a clear view of the city that held him in its belly. He had to admit, the raiders never came so far before. This new attack, even if not entirely successful, proved how easy breaching the Kaladian walls could be. Over the din of screams and the howling of the two brothers as they severed limbs and killed the fleeing people, Riel recognized the thundering sound of camels. The mounted soldiers approached.

He watched them arrive, edging his camel closer to the battle. One warrior stood out among the shadowy forms. The soldier wore the same muted grays as all the others, colors that blended with shadows, yet he fought with a sickening wrath. His blade shone wet and black with blood. He mowed down one of the king's high guards. The stringy warrior's fluid movements awed Riel; the soldier appeared to anticipate every attack, each dodge and feint. The Kaladian man cut down another high guard and charged through the remainder. *He is coming for me.*

The soldier shouted orders over his shoulder, a sign of his high rank. He rode forth, his mount wailing for blood. Riel drew his scimitar and hunched over his camel, kicking it toward the attack. The two crashed at each other, their camels rearing in the last moment. Swords struck, screeching their edges grating together. Riel's gaze caught on the mass of daggers the soldier wore at his belt. He sensed a pale light in the dark man's eyes, a glint he'd read about in the tomes back home. As the soldier broke away, grunting with disgust, he again chased his king.

This time, the captain succeeded. Tustin, Dalin and the rest of the mercenary army began to retreat. They galloped down the wide, main street, racing through the open gates of the first wall. Riel kept time with the two brothers. They bypassed the outer city, the fields of jindi and palms and the pastures of goats and sheep. *So much like home,* Riel realized. *Too much. We used to be one people, but now...* His ponderings trailed off. Foam frothed from his camel's mouth when they approached the second wall. The gates were closing, something that hadn't happened during their raids. The mass of Klemish men exited quickly, out into the night and the shadows of the dunes.

"Thank the one God!" Riel shouted. He lived; he survived his king's bizarre attack on their enemy. The captain held no illusion that it would end though. This strange massacre proved a beginning to the dark king's plans. Riel wished to be back home, safe in his wife's arms. He wondered if choosing D'atham's path might prove a better route. Queen Ashandera, ill as she was, never once made war. Her pursuits lay in bettering the city, in sustaining the resources they possessed. The captain questioned his loyalty as he chased his king back to their camp, to the tents and the inevitable beating he knew would come for pulling Tustin away too soon.

Chapter Eight: The Council

Raynier awoke alone. He stared for a long while at the emptiness in the bed beside him. As the morning dragged on in silence, he decided to get up and check for Shahzar in the bathing room. It was empty. A candle sat on the table beside the mirror. He carried it to the window to light it and sing the morning prayers. In the middle of his hymn, the door opened. Turning, he frowned at the servant. He finished his prayer and stood up to wait for whatever news she was bearing.

"Bishop," Inell began in an unsteady voice. "There's a council meeting and I'm to prepare you to attend." Inell was plain, dressed in the common browns of servants. The long skirt and heavy blouse she wore shrouded her body.

"It is forbidden, Inell," he said. The Shan-Sei hadn't been included in the formal workings of the council since the Division. It worried him and he still feared the temple would be destroyed — maybe this was just another way the council would go about it. Shahzar had left him in the night. Maybe she'd changed her mind about protecting him.

She nodded. "Many things that are forbidden her majesty allows. Many things she forces into being. She wants you present at the council meeting. You should go. She'll be angry if you do not."

The last thing he wanted was to anger Shahzar. He slipped on his boots. While he fastened the clasps on his robes, he eyed Inell. The little servant turned her back on him to take stock of the disarray on the desk. She bent to pick up some of the scroll sleeves that had fallen on the floor. "Such a mess," she muttered.

Raynier shook his head, wondering if the princess meant all she said the day before. He reached for the brown wrap and bound up his hair. He tied the silk belt over his robes, remembering when Shahzar had dropped it that first night. *Was it a mistake to tell her how I feel?'*

Dressed and ready, he followed Inell down the marble steps. She led him over mosaic-covered floors and beneath ceilings higher than the heavens. It was all a blur to him. Raynier tried to steady his breathing. The few servants they passed stopped and stared at him in wonder. His clothing revealed his identity, a temple priest, a member of Kaladia not usually allowed in the castle. They whispered about his presence.

At the council chamber door, Inell knocked three times, opened it and pushed the bishop inside. Raynier had only a moment to look back at the servant. She nodded at him to continue in and shut the wide door, sealing off his escape.

Heavy silence followed his entry. The bishop looked over the round table and the ornate tapestries that clung to the wall behind each seat. The unwavering stares of the council members seared through him; fourteen faces all stilled with shock, save one. Shahzar's eyes were downcast. *Why won't she look at me?* A wave of panic washed over him.

Shahmi stood, his leathery, brown face marred with pent-up rage. He beckoned Raynier to his side with one stiff hand. The bishop stumbled toward him, terrified. There was an empty seat beside the captain. Raynier took it and gazed again at Shahzar. Shahmi sat down and tapped his finger on the tabletop.

I am to be killed, was all he could imagine. He glanced over at Shahmi and frowned. The lithe, older man made a formidable picture with his close-cut, gray hair and scowling face and eyes. A jagged scar, whitened by age, cut deep into his left cheek and led down the side of his neck where it disappeared beneath the padded gray tunic he had on.

Tap, tap, tap.

Raynier's eyes widened when he saw the sheathed blades clinging to Shahmi's thick leather belt.

Tap, tap, tap.

He looked away, back to Shahzar. She was at the head of the table, her seat a bit higher than the others. Still, she wouldn't look at the bishop. Instead, she stood up and glowered down at all the others present in the room. Raynier wanted to see her eyes and know what was about to happen.

"The Klemish have penetrated the southern border," she announced. "They came in the night and killed thirty-three men, women and children. They have stolen goats and camels—burned homes." She glared at the council members, seeking their audience, but none would look at her. They were all staring at Raynier. The ancient man next to Shahzar pushed up his spectacles in order to see the priest better.

"Horlan," she said softly. The man didn't turn. She slapped the back of his head, making his turban fall askew into his eyes. "I'm speaking here! You will direct your attention to me!" The others turned their curious gazes from Raynier.

"But that's a priest." Horlan hissed. "The Shan-Sei aren't allowed in this room! It's forbidden! We must remember what those of the temple did."

She leaned forward, raising her hand.

Shahmi let out a tiny, snake-like hiss that sent shivers down Raynier's spine. The captain tapped his fingers on the table again. The bishop shifted in his seat.

Tap, tap, tap.

Shahzar's eyes flickered on her uncle for a moment. She slapped Horlan, this time across the old man's cheek. The harsh sound echoed in the wide room.

Raynier gasped. The others glanced at him briefly and returned their attention to Shahzar. They were all older than the princess, clearly in high positions, and yet she didn't seem to fear any of them.

As the meeting resumed, Raynier watched the red mark grow on Horlan's withered cheek. Each of Shahzar's fingers showed as plainly as her palm print. The old man didn't look at the bishop again.

"I want the guards to pursue the raiders immediately. This time, we won't let them go. From now on, when they attack, we'll hunt them down. Too long have we turned a blind eye on the Klemish. Too long have they crossed the outskirts and murdered our people with no recourse from our armies."

Shahmi stood. Raynier flinched. The captain bowed to his niece. "Your will is mine, my lady," he said softly. "I'll gather my men and pursue the band of raiders." With that, he crossed the room, his array of weapons clattering. When he closed the door behind him, Raynier breathed a sigh of relief.

"The next matter will be that of the aqueducts," said the round woman directly across from the bishop. "The recent rains have overflowed the storage facilities and the aqueducts are in dire need of repair."

"Eschelle, what do you recommend?" Shahzar called across the table.

A tall, sharp-nosed guild leader stood. She adjusted the blue sash over her shoulder and spoke. "Pontye said there's a new way to construct the aqueducts, with a material that won't decay. I'll need supplies from Masters Yashpal and Antirion." She nodded at both guild-masters respectively.

"I approve of this. Is anyone opposed?" Shahzar snapped.

The room remained silent. Tension lingered heavy in the air. Obviously, the princess was growing into her station too fast for many of the council members. Only one, Raynier noted, seemed to be smiling, taking in the meeting with a certain jovial air about him. He was a thick man. So large that he sat back from the table to provide room for his ample belly. His dull, black eyes went from Eschelle to Shahzar, then settled on Horlan. The portly man smirked when he stood up. "My will serves yours, Shahzar. I will give Eschelle all she requires."

"Thank you, Master Yashpal," Shahzar said.

Another man stood. He eyed Raynier, as most had when the priest entered the room. The ebony-colored man was a tower of muscle. The yellow sash over his shoulder blazed against his sanguine garb. He took in a deep breath. "The aqueducts will be my priority; the water they ration spares us all in times of drought..."

"And I thank you as well, Master Antirion. Go now, Eschelle, and begin the construction," Shahzar interrupted. She nodded at the man and then turned to the sharp-nosed woman again. "Use whatever means you require."

Eschelle stood, bowed and prepared to leave. She paused at the door to glance back at Raynier. Like all the others present, there was a glint of curiosity in her eyes.

"There are no more matters to be resolved," said the round woman as she rapped her stick against the table. "Does anyone wish to bring forth a new subject before we adjourn?"

Horlan leapt from his seat, an action that defied his bent, frail appearance. The red mark glowed on his cheek as he made himself heard, determined to put Shahzar on the spot. "I wish to bring up the matter of this priest!" He waved his gnarled hand in Raynier's direction. "It's forbidden to have him present. The council should remove him at once! He doesn't belong here and he isn't welcome. Does anyone oppose this matter?"

"I oppose," said Shahzar. She nodded at the round woman.

Raynier looked up at Shahzar. She was simply clad in a brown dress, her curly hair peeking from the bottom of the veil that covered it. Dark circles beneath her eyes hinted at her lack of sleep.

"The princess opposes; it will be noted. What is your reasoning?" The round woman leaned forward, watching Horlan, a smile threatening her lips.

"This priest is the new bishop, sent from the temple. He's come to this council as my guest so that he may better understand our goals." Shahzar kept her eyes on the speaker, her voice steady and emotionless.

The round woman nodded. She looked about the room. "Are there any others that oppose?" she asked, raising one brow.

The room was silent save for a few papers shuffled across the table and the scratch of the quills as the scribes scrawled out the meeting minutes. "Princess," Sheah began, "you have brought this priest into our council to learn. Is it your intent that he remains a part of us and attend each of its meetings hereafter?"

"That is my intent."

The round woman nodded. "Bishop Raynier," she began. The speech sounded rehearsed. "This is the council of Kaladia. Each of us represents a guild within the city. I am Sheah. I represent the guild of knowledge." She turned and directed her stick at the tapestry on the wall behind her seat. Raynier noted the symbol for the book of knowledge. "Antirion of the masons," she continued, using her stick to point out the ebony colored man with the yellow sash beside her. Antirion lowered his head, his black eyes sharp as a hawk's. "This is Machiel of the camel and horse guild and his partner, Rond, of the small livestock guild." She swept her stick over the two twin brothers in haste, which reflected the weight of importance they held. "Jaider of the courts, Vasuman of the fires, Tussar of the messengers, Geetha and Chitra who together manage the windmills and sun harvesters." Sheah aimed her stick at the portly man with his protruding belly. "And Yashpal of the wastes."

Yashpal spared a kind grin for Raynier and rubbed his chin, soaking up the moment. The princess was asserting herself in the strangest of ways, and the master of the wastes looked as though he couldn't wait to see what she would do next.

Sheah pointed out Horlan. There she paused, eyeing the bent man with a hint of disgust. "This is Horlan of the botanical guild." She pointed to the empty seat beside the bishop. "Shahmi represents the guild of the guards and foot-soldiers." She aimed for the other vacant seat beside Horlan's. "Eschelle represents the guild of water." She hesitated for a moment. "Is it your wish to enter this council to represent the temple and the Shan-Sei?"

Raynier turned to Shahzar, shocked at the offer. Her eyes remained downcast, leaving him in wonder. It was a strange plan. His induction into the council would give Raynier the opportunity to save the priests. "Yes. I will represent the temple and the Shan-Sei."

Horlan slammed his gnarled fist down onto the table before him, an angry snarl curling his upper lip.

Sheah nodded, giving him the floor to speak.

"And who do the Shan-Sei serve?" Horlan asked with bitterness. The bent, old man stared up at Shahzar with a vehement glare.

The princess raised her head, ignoring Horlan, and seemed to notice the bishop for the first time that morning. He saw the light in her eyes and his breathing caught in his throat. Within his thoughts he heard her voice softly say: *Come on, remember the answer; tell them as I told you to say it.*

Raynier hesitated, wondering if he'd imagined her voice tarrying in his mind. His brows rose as he gazed at Shahzar hoping for some other sign, but she offered none. "The Shan-Sei serve the creator and all the people of Kaladia," Raynier answered. The small glint of light in her eyes betrayed what she was and the untapped abilities she possessed as she turned away.

Horlan pursed his wrinkled lips. The mark of Shahzar's palm blazed on his cheek. "How do the Shan-Sei serve the people? They sit in the temple and pray to an idol. They do nothing of importance! Remove him from this room! I urge all of you to vote against this ridiculous breach between the separation of the temple and our government!"

Again, Shahzar spoke softly within Raynier's mind. *Tell them you will teach the people to read and to write.*

Raynier nodded at her. He let Horlan's words fall away without a tone of argument in his own when he answered. "It's true that the last bishop did not promote service to the people, but I will be different. I request, with the permission of the council and the princess, to send my priests amongst the people to teach all who wish it to read and to write."

Shahzar smiled. The remaining council members took in a long breath as one. Horlan's eyes fixed on the bishop and the ancient Master smiled, albeit faintly.

Sheah nodded her approval.

"I take back my proposal that he be removed on the condition that he does what he says," Horlan offered, but in a grim warning, he added, "put a time counter on his words! If he fails, let him be cast back into the shadows behind the temple walls from where he crawled."

Sheah knocked on the table before her, eyeing Horlan. The old man was mouthy and mean, and the speaker's disdain for him showed plainly in her disgusted expression. "Does anyone else oppose?"

Silence ensued and Raynier became a part of the council of Kaladia, the first Shan-Sei priest to do so since the city had divided. The meeting adjourned. Members left the room, muttering to each other while they filed out. Shahzar stood and traveled the opposite way around the table so that she passed by Raynier.

"Wait for Inell," she whispered, her eyes ahead, as she walked out of the chamber.

Soon the squat servant appeared and filled the crook of her arm with the scrolls left near Shahzar's seat. She forced a dry smile at the bishop. "Follow me," she said and turned to go. Inell led Raynier a different way through the castle. He lost sense of what direction they took as they passed arch after arch in the lower halls. At one point, they skirted a window by the castle gardens, before turning down an unlit corridor.

Inell shuffled along in front of him, tracing the side of the wall with one pudgy finger. Raynier stopped, a strange sense of dread washing over him. Surely, she wouldn't allow Shahmi to kill him now, not after what just happened. "Where are you taking me?" he called.

His voice echoed in the corridor. Inell turned and her eyes were less wide, her face calmer than usual. "Milady has asked that I take you this way because she doesn't want the council to know you're here. They don't know you've been with her all this time. Only Shahmi and I know this. She likes her privacy."

They came out of a tunnel below the marble stairs. Raynier entered Shahzar's room and found her seated at her desk, studying her papers. She didn't turn or move to acknowledge either of them. Inell dropped the day's scrolls in the usual place and left without a word.

"You're free to go, Raynier. The council will protect you and the temple now." She stood up and brushed her hair back from her shoulders. "You don't need my protection any longer." She forced a smile that expressed her hope to be done with the ordeal.

"Do you want me to go?" he asked, dreading the answer.

"You're a danger to me," she began. "You cloud my judgment; make my reactions slow, for I'm always thinking of you."

A crease appeared between his dark brows. He'd not expected that at all. Raynier crossed the distance between them in hurried steps. He reached out and took her hand. "Give me one more night."

She bit at her bottom lip, contemplating her answer. "Sometimes I like the way you look at me," she said in a breathless whisper. Shahzar pulled her fingers from his.

Raynier sighed, afraid she was going to turn, but her hands trailed up to his turban, tugging it free. She took a step closer, the gold flecks in her dark eyes catching the light. Shahzar touched his hair, tentatively at first, and ran her fingers through it, caressing his temples and finally letting her palms rest against his cheeks.

Raynier felt afire as he had the first moment he saw her, the moment he'd described her to Toman as beautiful. She'd smiled directly at him then and he knew that he loved her, knew that she was meant for him, a gift from Ishas. "Let me stay," he whispered against her cheek as she leaned up to kiss his neck. Her hands found their way to a clasp on his robes. Soon the garment fell away. Her fingers trailed over the hairs on his chest. Raynier couldn't breathe. He couldn't hold himself back from her.

She drew in a sharp breath when he grasped her shoulders and pressed her against the desk. Her body tensed. She started to push him away but stopped. Gilt-brown eyes awash with curiosity, she leaned up to kiss his mouth, and he met her lips hungrily. Her hands slid down his sides and into his pants, forcing them away.

He lost control of his breathing once more. Inkbottles teetered as he pressed against her. Raynier pushed up her skirts and moved his hands down the back of the long, feminine undergarments she wore. Her skin felt cold against his warm fingers. They stared into each other's eyes, speechless as he slid the fabric from her. When he thrust against her again, their naked bodies joining, Shahzar closed her eyes.

Bottles of ink slammed into each other before they rolled off the desk onto the carpet. The heat of his body met the cold of hers and Raynier held still. She gasped and tightened her fingers on his waist, forcing him down hard, crushing papers beneath her. Scrolls still sealed within sleeves clattered as they, too, fell on the floor.

At last, Raynier thought, *she's mine*. It was a moment he didn't think possible, one he dreamed of since meeting her. Shahzar moaned in his mouth when he kissed her harder. He pulled her against him, forcing himself into her. The madness that swam in his thoughts, his heady desire for her overwhelmed him.

Shahzar urged him closer with each assault, her breathing slight and shallow. Her fingers pressed into his back and slid lower until she gripped his buttocks. Her mouth left his. She arched her back. Raynier held her hips, pulling her against him. She cried out, and his control slipped away. It was over before it had begun.

Shahzar released her hold on him, her eyes reflecting shock. She lay atop her desk, chest heaving and her body trembling against his where they touched. She turned away and covered her face with her palms.

He stepped back, ashamed, unable to face her. Raynier knelt to pick up the bottles, the sleeves, the papers, anything to avoid her gaze should she choose to look on him. Papers crunched and message sleeves rolled. Her hand came against his back, tracing a looping pattern there. He froze.

-o.O.o-

"Raynier, please go into my bed and warm the covers for me." She watched him retreat, her body tingling, her mind racing with the moment. "How did this happen?" she whispered. Shahzar placed the inkbottles on the desk. Then she carefully rolled each scroll and slid them into their fallen sleeves. She turned to study the closed bed-curtains before placing the scrolls on the desk. She couldn't see Raynier, but she felt him watching her. Shahzar took in a deep breath and closed her eyes. She slipped past the curtains into the bed, into his arms and the warmth.

"I did not mean for it to happen that way," Raynier said.

Shahzar studied him, a soft smile playing at her lips. Her voice sounded surprisingly calm when she spoke. "We have our whole lives to regret. Let this not be a day we think of when we do." She leaned over to kiss him, and he flinched. Shahzar frowned. She turned her head and pressed her lips against his ear to whisper. "Show me in what way you meant for it to happen. Please."

Chapter Nine: The Kaladian

Riel paused beside the gnarled bilsaberry tree to stare up at the Kaladian soldier hanging from wrist leathers against its trunk. The sunset blared behind the branches like fire, making the gory sight glow like the some hellish nightmare. "It's you," he whispered, though he doubted the man heard him. "You came at me in the city."

The soldier cracked his swollen eyes open and Riel cringed. The fluidity, the grace in battle with which the tortured man once moved would never come again. The captain had watched as Tustin sliced small gashes in the Kaladian's flesh. He stood, not ten paces away, when King Aberweir smashed the limb across the Kaladian's knees, crushing both.

"You're strong," Riel called out, approaching the soldier, his boots whispering over the loose, golden sand. "But if I were you, I'd just die. Tustin wants to break you. The questions he asks serve no purpose."

The Kaladian remained motionless, blood dribbling down his leathery skin. Riel looked for the light in the man's eyes, wondering if what he'd seen in Kaladia had been a musing of his imagination. The soldier's body, naked and battered, still showed signs of power. Signs, Riel knew, Tustin wanted to destroy.

Riel traced the tender flesh by his own right eye, cringing. *At least I only took one blow*, the Klemish captain thought. A low hissing sound drew his attention to the tortured soldier's face. The Kaladian's lips parted; his teeth clenched.

"You sound like a snake," Riel commented. He took a few more steps until he stood beneath the tortured soldier. New gashes stood out, red and wet, across the man's brown belly. Still, he did not speak. Riel guessed he felt too much pain to form words.

The Klemish captain glanced over his shoulder, across a flat of sand at the camp and his army gathered around the fires. Palms swayed in the building night breeze, their shadows lengthening by the minute. Tustin and Dalin had gone with their mercenaries to burn the remaining bodies. Plumes of acrid, black smoke marred the evening sky to the west. "They killed the soldiers with you," Riel muttered when he turned back. "All of them. Dalin went over each one and drew his mark on their faces with his blade."

The Kaladian blinked, his eyes swollen a bit more than Riel's, but clarity starting to shine in his pupils. His body twitched violently, then ceased.

Riel shook his head in disgust. "I can help you," he mumbled. He doubted once more if the soldier could hear him. "I know you're tired and you want this to end. Do you want that?" He reached up and touched the Kaladian's bloody arm.

The soldier flinched at the contact, accustomed to the coming pain.

"Are you the last Shan-Sei?" Riel asked. "Tell me and I'll end your life."

The Kaladian's eyes widened as much as they could, given their state. His trembling lips parted and he grunted, trying hard to find his voice after so many days of screaming. "There...are...no Shan-Sei," he rasped. "They left...after the... Division."

"I saw the light in your eyes. Don't lie to me. Tell me the truth and I'll end you. You want to die. How could you not? I would."

The Kaladian closed his eyes.

Riel shrugged and turned to leave. The Klemish captain wanted to go home so bad it hurt. He wanted to hold Euphenia close and tell her he loved her. This war made no sense. The atrocities Tustin and Dalin committed weighed on the captain's soul. His boots crunched in the dry sand as he retreated toward the fires.

The hiss sounded again.

Riel debated ignoring it, but compassion always weakened him. He glanced back, hoping the Kaladian hadn't opened his lightless eyes. Disappointment greeted him in those pained, brown eyes surrounded by raw, bruised flesh.

"Please...end it...now," the Kaladian rasped out.

Riel rushed to the tree. He fumbled in his pockets. *It might be me one day. Tustin could turn at any moment and I would hang there, beaten, crushed, broken and praying for death.* "I give you mercy," Riel murmured, holding the vial up. The Kaladian suckled at it, draining away the yellowy liquid. "I'm sorry I could not do more. Our people...are the same."

The vial came away empty and the Kaladian closed his eyes and shivered. "I wish she...could have heard me...say it once..."

"What?" Riel knew the poison would spare little time in taking effect.

"My niece..." the soldier sputtered, saliva eking from the corner of his mouth.

"What is your name, soldier? Maybe I can get word to her for you." Riel's mind swam with options. There were ways to send messages through the Jondah traders.

"Shahmi..." His voice cut as his lungs labored against the effects of death. "...Galkwin."

Riel stood by him, regret filling his chest, flooding his senses. "By Daumion, I cannot believe who you are, what this means..."

Shahmi's last breath came out in a soft sigh. He patted the dead man on his bloodstained arm, relieved that the Kaladian had not lived long enough to offer him a message. Riel turned an eye over the dunes, disgusted by what he'd become. As he started for the camp, his legs felt heavier and his heart screamed at him to abandon the crazed king. "If I live through this," he promised, "I will swear fealty to my queen."

Chapter Ten: Back to the Temple

Long before dawn, Shahzar clung to Raynier's hand. The two walked through the dark, arched halls. The princess kept her gaze trained on the way ahead, ready to withdraw her fingers from his should anyone cross their path. She led him back to the beginning, to the castle gates and his freedom. Her hair hung free and he kept glancing at her. She felt self-conscious for the first time in her life.

"I'm ashamed," Raynier began. "When you came to Toman in the temple that day, I stood by him because I wanted to withdraw as a candidate for the post of bishop. Had you not come, had I not seen you and known I could lie beside you for the rite, I would have remained a humble priest."

"Rest assured in your decision," she said, her cheeks burning at his words. "For had another priest come in your place that man would be dead now. Shahmi would have destroyed the temple. By your intentions toward me, you saved it." Shahzar shook her hair from her shoulders nervously.

He frowned at her, his words contradicting his expression. "I love you, Shahzar. I've loved you from that first moment you smiled at me through the window in the temple. I'll always love you."

She looked away, out over her city. Its people were still in their beds. The heavy silence of early morning clung to the air, and she wondered what it would be like to hear them all singing the Shan-Sei prayers as one. The princess thought it possible. *The old ways need to be brought back. Belief in Ishas will strengthen our patron Goddesses' protection over my city. It will unify the people. If I can bring back the old ways, the old priests, the dark power, then the Klemish raids would stop*

The white griffon statues atop the gate columns flanked Shahzar and Raynier. The princess let her gaze trail over them as she struggled for the appropriate way to dismiss Raynier. She knew the words he wanted to hear. Shahzar felt his eyes pulling at her, begging for those words, words she must keep locked inside. Shahmi had warned her about getting too close to anyone.

"I'm in love with you," he said. "Does it mean nothing?" His voice trembled with an edge of desperation.

"There are many pieces to my heart," she began, hating the coldness in her voice, "and you hold but one small facet. That's all I can afford to give you." She stole a glance at his face before looking away, afraid of the pain shimmering in his eyes. Her hand left his and she turned to go.

She walked at a gentle pace, holding back her emotions. When she was sure he couldn't see her, Shahzar ran. The princess raced back through the halls, her shoes tapping. Servants had risen to light the lamps and open the curtains to the morning sun, and she dodged them without a backward glance.

She passed the old murals of queens, slowed when she entered the final hall and stopped at the marble steps that led to her bedchamber. Out of breath, her heart fluttering, she closed her eyes. "Help me to do what is right, Ishas," she gasped.

Her hand went instinctively to the gold chain hidden beneath her dress, and she tugged it free. The shapely charm at the necklace's end fell against the blood-red fabric of her dress. Shahzar closed her fingers over the copper talisman. Her skin crawled. The metal felt far too icy. A wave of dizziness set in and Shahzar's breath caught.

"Each time you call for me, I feel stronger." The whispery voice hung by her ear, echoing in an unnatural way.

Shahzar let the amulet go and grabbed the banister. She climbed up the marble steps, her mind focusing, her breath slowing to a calmer state. The voice worried her. No Goddess had spoken to her before Raynier. "Have I gone mad?" she muttered as she pulled open the door. Shahzar surveyed her room to be sure she was alone.

The cold set in, enveloping her in its familiar hold. She climbed into her bed and lay in the area where Raynier had slept. The sheets were scented with his soft, smoky smell. She breathed in. His warmth that once clung to the fabric faded, leaving her as alone as she'd always been. She shivered, her eyes locked on the opening in the curtains. "What have I done?" she whispered.

-o.O.o-

For a long time, Raynier stood between the griffon statues. He watched the merchants far below the steps of the castle as they set up their tables in the morning twilight. The guards at the gates were watching the city as well. The quiet morning filled his heart with emptiness. Shahzar had left him in such a cold way. The bishop took the stairs slowly, his eyes on the temple only a few blocks away. For the first time in his life, he had no desire to sing the morning prayers. He passed the merchants without turning his head, unwilling to meet their curious looks, and made his way back to the temple, disappearing within its walls.

He passed through the courtyard and along the flat, stone paths that circled the inner workings of the Shan-Sei temple. Most of the priests had risen by then and stood gathered in the worship area to sing in unison. Raynier trudged toward the hall, attempting to return to the life he knew. He entered through a side door and paused, looking over the faces of the priests under his care. They sat on the lines of mottled, wooden benches, their turban-covered heads bowed in silence. It made a neat, orderly scene: the men and boys all in black robes, joined in their faith. The air in the room smelled of smokewood and lemon incense. Another scent mingled with the two more prominent ones, that of the Tharthen flowers that bloomed in the temple gardens. Raynier was home, but he felt no joy in it.

Endela pushed his way past a few of the older priests and stopped to bow, his watery eyes showing with emotion. "Bishop," he began. "I will pray that she conceives a girl so you will not have to return to her."

Though his words were heartfelt, and not meant to insult, they stung Raynier. He held out his hand and let Endela pat it in reverence. "I'll need a few hours alone this morning to reflect," he explained. Without waiting for a response, he turned and went out the door. He wasn't ready to forget her yet. He passed along the flagstone path through the inner gardens of the temple, hardly noticing the blooming yellow flowers that used to set him at ease. Behind him, the priests' voices filtered from the worship hall. The sounds echoed across the high walls around the temple and filled him with a sense of purpose.

Raynier made his way to his room. He'd kept the same chamber since his induction. The Shan-Sei were humble no matter their station. In a way, he was thankful for the simplicity of the small space. The minimal room held all he needed: a cot, an undersized wooden table, a worn chair, and a closet for his robes and dark pants. He lit the candle at the window and prayed to the morning sun. His voice cracked, but he forced himself to go on. The words gave him strength. He reached down, out of habit, for the tiny idol of Ishas and smiled. Shahzar possessed it now.

Later that morning, he conducted the circle meeting with the higher priests. "I bring news from the castle," he announced. "The princess has need of us. She has made a place for the Shan-Sei in the Guild Council. In exchange for that representation, I have promised that our priests will go out among the city and teach the people to read and write."

At the news, many priests reacted with nervousness, some twisting their mouths and others fidgeting in their seats. Many had never been beyond the temple walls, and others only remembered the outer world from a child's view. Raynier knew what they were feeling. He also felt unsure, but it had to be done.

"Ishas has come to me in a dream. She spoke to me." Raynier's eyes pierced each priest, fixing them with a solemn gaze. A few gasped at his words and made the holy sign of the circle above their foreheads. They shuffled anxiously while the bishop gathered his words.

"She wants us to spread her teachings, to expand her followers. The more souls that pledge themselves to our lady, the stronger She will become. When we go among the Kaladians, we will teach them who they are, that they are Shan-Sei. Bring with you the holy writ and give to each man, woman and child a talisman of our goddess so that they can revere her and learn the morning prayers." Raynier paused to judge their faces. They still looked scared, but now, they had a purpose.

-o.O.o-

In the beginning, the people shied away from the darkly clad priests. As time wore on, the citizens began to gather in the marketplaces to hear the Shan-Sei priests speak. It happened slow, a wave from a merchant when a temple priest passed his stand, the sign of the circle made over an old woman's brow, the hundreds of talismans worn across people's chests—all small changes reaching for a higher goal. With each step, the being beneath the Shan-Sei temple stirred. Ishas, a great goddess that fell when her people divided, had nearly awakened.

Each night, tired from wandering about the city and struggling to teach stubborn merchants their letters, Raynier would collapse on his cot and fall into dreams of Shahzar. Her gilt-brown eyes haunted him, as did the memory of their shared kisses and the feel of her fingers rubbing at his temples and through his hair.

The weekly council meetings brought him no solace. Each time he attended, he would wait for her to look his way. Not once did she reward him. She would answer his questions if pressed, but her eyes remained downcast. It tore at him to see her leave each time, but he didn't have the courage to follow her down the hall and beg for her attention.

A month passed since his last night with Shahzar. Inell came down from the castle and found Raynier in the temple's gardens. She stood in front of him, her hands crossed over the rich, earth-colored dress she wore. Her eyes were as wide as always when she addressed Raynier. "Milady requests books."

"Books?" He sat on a stone bench and watched the small white butterflies that frequented the flowers along the path. "What kind of books?"

"Books about the Shan-Sei and Ishas. She said you would know what to send." Inell pursed her lips and waited for the bishop to get up, clearly anxious to be on her way. The servant swept her gaze around the gardens and across the homely temple walls.

"Did she send a note?" he asked, unable to hide the anguish in his voice.

"A note, Bishop?" Inell cleared her throat and looked past him. "No. She sent me... for the books. She assumed you knew exactly which books she desired, as I said."

He frowned and stood up. It wasn't what he meant, but he didn't feel comfortable explaining himself to Inell. "Come down to the worship hall, and I'll choose some from the rear study."

"Yes, Bishop." She trailed him along the meandering path, but stopped short when he knelt to pick one of the bright, yellow-gold flowers that lined the walk. Raynier saw her tilt her head to the side as she spied on him.

In the study at the rear of the worship hall, Inell shadowed Raynier. Her eyes narrowed as the bishop slid the single Tharthen flower into the midst of a tome. He placed the book on top of five others and held them out to the servant. "Tell her..." He stumbled over his words, frowned and began once more. "Tell Shahzar her will is mine and that I promise to serve her in any way she asks."

Inell nodded, her gaze focused on the flower hanging from the pages of the book. "I will, Bishop." She spun around and headed down the stairs. She wobbled down the aisle toward the open, main doors. After she left him, he wished he'd said more.

The next morning, as Raynier lay in his bed, he thought he heard someone singing the morning prayers. Twilight edged around his small chamber and he wondered who would sing the prayers so early. The gentle, feminine voice carried on the wind, reaching into his open window and fading against the brick and mortar walls. Each morning that followed, Raynier listened and found it just before the time he would sing his prayers. He hoped the voice belonged to Shahzar.

The weekly council meeting moved slowly. Shahzar stood and made her way to the door before the others. This time, Raynier felt determined to speak to her. He followed, cutting off Yashpal when the wide man hobbled for the exit.

The bishop didn't have far to go to find her. Shahzar stood by an arched window that overlooked the soldier's barracks. She watched the foot-soldiers practice their fighting in the dusty yard. Sunlight showed on her face, and Raynier saw the pain in her eyes. He hoped she'd turn her head and see him, if only for a moment.

Shahzar dropped her hands against the sides of her heavy, sanguine dress and clenched her fists. The black and gold veil that barely hid her straightened hair drew his eyes to her face when she tugged it free. Raynier hurried toward her, his heart racing.

"It has been a month and a half since we sent Shahmi into the wastelands," she said.

He stopped short when he saw the young man she addressed. His hair was cut short in the manner of all foot-soldiers and though he had dark skin as most Kaladians did, the man had a narrow face. His clothes appeared finer than that of a lowly soldier, though the muted colors matched the standard uniforms. He pushed off from the archway and moved closer to the princess, his shifty, green eyes sweeping over Raynier before he nodded at Shahzar.

"Someone wants to speak to you it seems," the young man said.

She glanced over her shoulder at the waiting priest. Their eyes met for the first time in weeks. Her mouth tensed. "What is it, Raynier?"

"May I have a moment with you?" he asked.

The younger man came between them, cutting off his view and when he'd passed, Shahzar turned back to the window. The soldier whispered to her and leaned against the opposite arch, eyeing Raynier with distrust. He seemed hidden in the shadows, spying with the impatient manner of a stealthy guard dog.

"Can it wait?" she spoke to the glass, to the soldiers that danced and parried across the yard.

"If that is your wish." Raynier backed away. He leaned on the far wall and watched as the young man emerged. Handsome in a swarthy, blatant way, the soldier moved as if he knew his looks were irresistible. He pressed his body to the window, looking into Shahzar's face with a heady gaze as she spoke to him. Nodding, he held up his hand to lightly touch her shoulder before he started off at a quick walk. As he passed the bishop, Raynier noticed the scars the young man bore, one across his forehead and another on his right cheek. He looked rough and overconfident when he sneered at the bishop. The young man disappeared through the side door, crossing the yard and calling to the soldiers lined up by the barracks.

"What is it?" Shahzar stared at him then, her face cold. She held her veil in both hands, twisting the fabric in opposite directions.

He crossed the hall to stand before her, unsure if she'd allow him to take her hand or get nearly as close as the younger man did. His mind screamed out that the soldier had to be her lover, her new consort. Raynier opened his mouth to speak and stammered over his words. "I wanted to know...if you are well."

"Mmm." She nodded, not bothering to answer his question. "I'm sending a band of men to find Shahmi. He should have come home by now." She let one side of her veil slip from her fingers and touched the glass, turning her attention once more to the soldiers. "If anyone can find him, Irlecain can." She tapped the glass, indicating the soldier that just left her company. She backed away. "Is there anything else, Raynier?"

He frowned and shook his head no. All the words he'd bottled up refused to come out.

"It's good to see you..." she hesitated, "... away from the others." Shahzar bit her bottom lip, ready to take her leave when he reached for her hand. Her fingers were colder than he remembered. She held still, her body visibly tensing at the familiarity. She jerked away then, leaving him with her veil.

Chapter Eleven: Uncle's Return

Two weeks passed as quickly as a sandstorm cuts down a dune and melts it to nothing. Raynier spent his time tutoring the merchants and their children or holding sermons in the streets. The bishop stood with Endela in the city's herder district when a procession passed. "Hisa will learn them in time," he reminded Endela.

His mousy advisor balanced from one foot to the other. He cast a dissatisfied glance at the camel merchant's unruly child and sighed. "I will try again." Endela knelt and repeated the letters to Hisa. The boy fidgeted.

"That's good Hisa, keep at the…" In mid-sentence, Raynier froze, his words stolen by the oncoming procession. The soldiers Shahzar sent to find Shahmi were returning. The young foot-soldier, Irlecain, his face bloodied, led them. A body swayed across his saddle, lit up by the bright, morning sunlight. As they passed Raynier, Irlecain's camel balked and the dead man's head lolled to one side. Raynier gasped. Shahmi's lifeless eyes were no less stark in death as they had been in life. The open gashes across the leathery face and arms attested to his torture.

That night, as he lit the offering candle, Raynier whispered a prayer for Shahmi's soul. He pulled the gray, wool covers over his body and drifted into a light sleep. Long after the triple moons made their passes, he awoke to the sound of Endela's chattering. The advisor's voice raised three octaves as he argued with whoever approached him in the hall. Still half-asleep, he thought the woman's voice sounded familiar.

"I seek the bishop's council. I will not be denied!" she cried out.

Endela's voice echoed closer to Raynier's room, his boots clunking on the flagstone path as he approached, pursuing the intruder. "Lady, the hour is late..."

A thud and the shuffle of feet against stone followed by Endela's small cry startled Raynier so much that he stood and opened his door. Shahzar stood outside. She'd come dressed in black with silver trim, the garments of a Shan-Sei priest's robes, only tailored in a feminine way. Her straightened, long, black hair bore one scarf-like tie that held the length gathered at the small of her back. She held her fist over Endela.

The fallen advisor's bloodied lip dripped onto his black robes. His wide, mousy eyes went from the princess to the bishop in shock.

"Shahzar?"

She turned to face him. Her fist dropped to her side, and she pushed past Raynier into his small chamber. He breathed deep the scent of her.

Endela stood and wiped his lip on his sleeve. He looked down at the blood, gasped and started to retreat.

"I'm sorry; please forgive her," he mumbled before he shut the door on his advisor. He set the bar in place to keep out any intruders, his heart racing. The bishop turned and sucked in a heavy breath. Shahzar sat down on the cot, her body trembling. Raynier went to his desk and pushed in the chair. He ran his hand through his loose hair and went to stand in front of her.

"My uncle is dead," she said solemnly. Her eyes looked drawn and dark circles hung below them. "Be silent and hold me close this night. I'm colder than the winter wind after the moons have passed. If you don't hold me, I'll die from this sorrow." She sniffled, but no tears showed in her eyes.

Raynier came to her side and placed his blanket over her shoulders. She scooted further into his cot and collapsed. He lay down beside her, careful not to move lest he fall off the edge. The bishop pulled her into his arms and remained quiet as she requested.

Shahzar shivered and closed her eyes. She curled her body close to him and he felt the curve of her belly pressing into his own. The last night they were together, she'd been pure muscle. This softness felt new. Raynier smiled, realizing she carried his child. After Shahzar fell asleep, he let his hand slip down to her belly, waiting for some sign of life within.

Dawn came and both rose to sing the morning prayers together. Raynier marveled at how a woman's voice danced within the temple walls. "It was you," he whispered when they stood. "Each morning I could hear your voice." That she'd begun that rite of faith encouraged him.

"Be silent." She touched her belly. "You have done all you can for me. Now I must avenge my uncle." With those few words, she left him standing there alone.

As his door shut, he thought of her voice mingled with his during the prayer. *Shahzar is changing*, he mused. The robes she wore defied the customs of her station. By singing the prayers, she denied the separation of temple and council. The light in her eyes when she left concerned Raynier more. The dark power within her continued to grow. "I fear for you," he whispered.

-o.O.o-

Inell came the next night to escort the bishop to Shahzar's chamber. Raynier felt too afraid he'd say something to make her angry, something that would cause her to send him away. Shahzar silently led the bishop to her bed and curled around him. She rested her cheek on his chest and closed her eyes. In minutes, she fell asleep. He waited until her breathing became regular before he stroked her cheek and hair.

In the morning, they rose and prayed together. When they stood up in front of the window, she reached for his hand. Side by side, they watched the sky light up. The sun rose over the wastelands beyond the city's walls. The two still stood there when Inell came in. The servant began to run Shahzar's bath. The princess paused for a while, holding the bishop's hand, but suddenly she broke away, escaping to her bathing chamber.

Raynier sat on her bed, unsure of what to do. When she emerged, he gaped at her clothing, plain trousers and a padded, beige tunic. Inell chased after her to tie up her long, curly hair with leather thongs. That the curls remained worried Raynier. He knew she preferred her hair straightened. She looked like a foot-soldier. "Where are you going?"

Inell turned on him, shaking her head. Her wide eyes sent a warning that silence was best at the moment.

Shahzar said nothing.

"You're not going out there? Not after the Klemish?" he pressed. These same raiders killed her uncle; the same men slaughtered villagers in exchange for a herd of sheep or goats.

Inell tied off the last strip of leather and jumped when someone knocked at the door. She scurried away to answer it with yet another warning look when she passed the bed.

"You are the heir to the throne," he pleaded. "You can't go out into the sands like a guard. You can't put your life in danger, not like this, not—"

Shahzar raised her hand, silencing the bishop. "I can do whatever I feel I must."

Inell escorted a man into the room. The soldier carried a trunk. Raynier frowned. He recognized the young man as the same foot-soldier that brought Shahmi's body through the streets of the city. His hair, shorn close to the scalp, almost to the point of baldness, indicated his mourning for the loss of his captain.

Irlecain shot Raynier a cold look, and opened the inlayed chest. He began to dress Shahzar in the armor that lay within. That task done, he pulled out a long, curved sword. "This was your uncle's," he said, his tone solemn and hushed.

Shahzar drew the sheathed blade. She held it aloft as if it weighed nothing, her eyes sparkling with the white light that only Raynier seemed to notice. "Cain," she said as she replaced the scimitar. "It's time for us to go." She left without another word to him.

Chapter Twelve: The Hunt

Irlecain rode beside Shahzar, his heart racing with regret and the overwhelming feelings he held back for her. Their mounts grumbled and brayed at each other; both camels accustomed to stepping in time yet still determined to move ahead. Their comical race to be first reminded Irlecain of the way he and Shahzar were when they fought. She tried to outdo him at any given chance. Most times, she succeeded. The fluidity of her movements during practice and on the battlefield likened to Shahmi's. Uncle and niece possessed an unnatural grace. Each appeared to anticipate their opponent's next action with an uncanny knack. Irlecain spent hours mulling over their talent, but never addressed it. *Certain mysteries in life should not be questioned.*

The sun beat down on the dunes, blinding the troops. The soldiers that followed pulled the fabric of their scarves up to shield their noses and mouths. Searing winds crossed before them, blurring the horizon with shifting sand. Irlecain squinted at the bright, blue sky above and let his mind empty. He waited to feel the way.

Shahzar's leg pressed against his. He flinched at the close touch and turned to look at her. She watched him, her amber-colored eyes heavy with revenge. He knew it was the camel's doing, that she would never move against him on purpose unless battle called for it. "To the south," he offered. His sense called him that way. The trait for finding lost things came from his father. Shahzar asked him to explain it many times. He tried to show her what it felt like, but she would only shake her head, clearly awed by his talent, and unable to fathom its plausibility.

"South?" she asked, a hint of doubt in her cold voice.

"I feel the calling to the south," he confirmed.

She jerked at her camel's reins and her leg moved away from his. He sucked in a dry breath and pulled the fabric over his mouth as well.

"Lead me," she barked.

Irlecain girded his mount and the two camels galloped together, racing across the empty wastelands, their troops following in line. Sand flew behind them. For hours, they chased his invisible trail.

When dusk came and the dunes rose higher, like looming monsters shadowed by the impending darkness, Shahzar slid down from her camel. She patted his neck in a familiar gesture that held little affection. "Still south?" she asked.

Irlecain nodded, out of breath from the ride. "I can feel them just there," he pointed. "Three days' ride at least." He dismounted and led his camel to a collection of dry brush. "We'll rest here and start again when the moons come into unison." He said it to confirm what he knew she already desired.

"Yes," Shahzar said. "I won't stop until I find them, until I kill them." She handed her mount's reins to Irlecain, turned on her heels and walked away.

He watched her go, her long, black braid swaying at her back. Behind him, he heard the others catch up. *Is this the last time I'll be so close to you?* Her lithe body, its womanly curves showing only slightly beneath her soldier's garb, tempted him. Shahzar, his friend, his princess, made her way to the shadows beneath a dune. She sat down, crossing her legs and closing her eyes to rest and wait. Irlecain dared not go close to her.

-o.O.o-

On the third night, they rode out, pressing their war camels harder than before. Darkness gave the desert an eerie feel. The sands looked pale, tinged with blue shadows as the first and second moons passed over the third. The sky lit up with a blue-gray light. Irlecain and Shahzar kept their pace far ahead of their entourage. "I feel scouts coming," he warned.

Shahzar said nothing for a time. She eased her mount to a steady walk, waving in signals to the men that followed. The two came around a gathering of palm trees and stopped. Klemish voices, garbled by distance and wine, drifted on the night breeze. Thin, wispy trails of smoke tainted the starry horizon. Irlecain let his camel have its way and the sturdy beast sidled against Shahzar's. He looked at her hands, curled tight around the reins and visibly trembling. "Let our men take them. Menes will be sure to let one live long enough to question."

Shahzar's lips pursed tight. Her eyes narrowed on the oasis in the distance. She sniffled once, and sighed. "I want to kill them, Irlecain. Let me do it."

He leaned across his saddle and gripped her arm. "You know I can't do that. Not now, not this time. Shahmi might have let you when we were in the ranks, but you will be queen. It's time you face that."

She shrugged off his hold. "If I were charging in with you at my side, Shahmi would let me."

"Stay back this time, Shahzar."

She looked away, out across the desert at the smoke and the inevitable battle.

Menes caught up to them first. The assassin, a friend of Irlecain's from his days in Bisura, jumped down from his camel. He strode over the sand with soundless steps, a man made of shadow in his black clothing. Only his eyes shined in the moonlight. The rest of his face lay hidden by wraps of cloth.

"Save her one. Spare no others. Make it silent," Irlecain ordered.

The assassin flagged down his chosen men, only five, all dressed in the same manner. They bowed before Shahzar, stood up and ran off into the shadows of the palms. Behind them, the night wind came stronger.

Irlecain edged his mount close to hers again. *Don't run into it*, he warned in silence. Her hands shook, her gaze cast on the palms. Both listened to the laughter, the raucous voices, waiting for silence to ensue.

"You can't understand how much I want to be there," she whispered.

"I loved him, too," he whispered back.

The princess grasped at her collar, tugging free the talisman of Ishas.

Irlecain leaned forward, curious. She muttered under her breath, and he felt a chill pass through his body. "Are you praying?" he gasped out in disbelief.

Her face changed, her lowered gaze making her appear to be in a trance. Shahzar didn't answer him. Her voice came out so softly that he couldn't make out her words.

He eased closer still and frowned. The language she spoke varied from Kaladian though he knew some words. "Is that Shan-Sei you're speaking?" He held out his hand, reaching for her arm. The wind danced around her mount, making sand curl up from the earth. Just as his outstretched fingers touched the armor covering her forearm, her camel balked. It reared up. Shahzar let go of the trinket and clenched the reins, driving her mount forward at full speed.

"Shahzar! No!" Irlecain's camel, too used to fighting alongside hers, gave chase. In the distance, the Klemish scouts became silent. *Menes did it,* he thought in a panic. *Why is she charging in there?*

When the princess reached the thick shrubs and palms that surrounded the oasis, he lost sight of her. It looked like the shadows reached out and sucked her within their darkness. "Come on," he ordered. "Come on, catch her!"

The first high-pitched cry sounded.

Irlecain slapped at the untrimmed palm leaves that blocked his view. The bushes and fallen growth crashed under his mount's steps. "Damn it, Shahzar!" he cried. "What have you done!"

Another man shrieked. Then another, and another.

Menes appeared beside himHis men flanked the assassin, but none could keep up with the camel as it charged and their shadows were soon lost in the dark. Fires in a clearing by the oasis well burned unattended, the bodies strewn beside them proof of the assassins' handiwork.

Irlecain searched in vain for some sign of Shahzar. "She's not in the trees," he muttered. "How could she move so fast?"

A familiar braying lured him past the edge of the palms where he found her rider-less war camel pawing at the sand. Its reins lay slack, the tasseled ends scraping the ground. More smoke rose behind a set of dunes and Irlecain saw the pointed tops of the tents. The entire Klemish army lay there and Shahzar's tracks led straight for it.

Panic clenched his heart. He kicked his camel hard, sending it rushing forth. Shahzar's indignant mount screamed its fury and followed. Irlecain didn't care if the others caught up to him. He didn't want to see what horror lay beyond those dunes. Visions crossed his mind; her eyes wide, stuck forever on the heavens, her body bloodied and her raven black hair all loose against the pale, moonlit sand.

He tuned out the screaming, the blood-curdling pleas for mercy. When Irlecain crested the dunes and looked down over the massacre, he couldn't believe the truth. Klemish soldiers lay in a clear path of death. Some appeared to have no wounds; others had died horribly from Shahzar's blade. Blood glittered in the moonlight, all colorless and wet.

"Shahzar!" he screamed. In the distance, a band of Klemish retreated north. *They're going back home, but how is this possible?'*

His camel slowed, and sensing its master's enemy, it trampled those men that lay dying. Irlecain still dreaded his friend's death. "She must be dead. There's no way she could survive this." He crossed through the camp and stopped at the edge, his mind racing with worry for her and the child she carried.

"Shahzar!" he cried.

The warrior looked up, her face splashed with blood, her sword lying beside her, drenched. Shahzar held fast to a line of leather rope, her eyes reflecting a dull sheen in the darkness. She stood up, swaying, and tugged roughly on the lead. Somewhere below her, in the shadows, a man grunted.

"What have you done?" he asked, his voice shaking. "Shahzar, what have you done here?"

Her jaw tightened, and she started to walk toward her mount. Wordless, she laced the lead over her camel's saddle, doubling the knot.

Irlecain dismounted and ran toward her. He glared at the prisoner tied to the end of her lead like an animal. More Klemish soldiers stood gathered in a huddle, their eyes wide and fixed on the princess. They made no attempt to attack or retreat. They remained there, as if waiting.

"Shahzar?" He caught up to her as she turned to make her way toward the onlookers. He stepped in time beside the princess, startled by her cold demeanor. "What are you doing?"

"He did it," she said in a voice that sounded nothing like her own. Shahzar waved her hand back at the man she'd tied up. "I saw it in his eyes. He killed Shahmi." She grabbed for a coil of rope at her hip and stopped, her body swaying once more.

Irlecain looked down at her hands and saw that they remained steady. Something felt wrong. The air caressed his face and chilled him to the core. Shahzar never spoke in such a hideous rasp before then. He tried to reason the change away and to convince himself that all those men had not died by her hand. *Impossible.*

He glanced at the huddle of Klemish soldiers remaining. Fear shone in their eyes, manifesting itself in their quivering mouths and the way they held their hands up in submission when Shahzar approached them. Irlecain squinted at the shadows behind the men and swore he could see them moving, although the Klemish prisoners remained still.

Chapter Thirteen: Aberweir

Days slowly turned into a week. Raynier anxiously awaited some word of Shahzar. He feared that she'd gone to her death, that he'd never see her again. The bishop had just finished tutoring a camel merchant who spoke with a lisp when a cheer broke out. People poured from their homes and lined the street to await the oncoming parade. The soldiers were returning. Raynier pushed his way through sweaty bodies all clad in cinnamons and reds. He found an opening and stopped at the edge of the street to watch. The individual cheers rose as one great sound that swept away all others. Merchants stopped calling out their wares and gawked at the procession.

The leader came into view, the bricked streets echoing behind her with the approach of more camels. Soon the line was just twenty paces from where Raynier stood. Shahzar's camel tossed its head proudly, braying in a raucous way at the onlookers. The princess appeared stoic atop her mount. She wore no helmet and the people knew her. Her wild hair blew back in the hot breeze, framing her face like an ebony mane. The bishop studied the thin line of her mouth, the tightness of her jaw, the coldness in her eyes. She wasn't looking at the people, only the road ahead, and the castle in the distance upon its hill.

At first he rejoiced, thinking only, *she's alive.* But, as she passed, Raynier saw the body. It dragged behind her mount, bound at the wrists by a rope attached to her saddle. He couldn't tell whether the man was alive or dead. The bishop sucked in a heavy breath when she passed and watched as more soldiers followed, dragging other prisoners behind them. There were ten in all, some running to keep up with their captors. Others had fallen, their limp bodies pulled across the road.

-o.O.o-

The following day, Endela came to Raynier in the circle room. "She's put them to death." His mousy eyes were solemn over the ill news he carried. "The princess put the noose over their heads with her own hands." He touched the yellowed bruise above his lip self-consciously. "I pray each night that she'll bear a daughter so you won't have to go back to her."

"Thank you." Raynier said. He looked up at the tapestries of The Division, at the embroidered rendering of Vonhadi and his seven followers, their arms upraised and the blackened earth encroaching on the forest beyond. *Oh Shahzar, what will become of you now?*

-o.O.o-

Four long days passed before Endela led Inell to the bishop with a look of foreboding. The servant's wide, brown eyes seared through Raynier. She waited until Endela left them to speak.

"The council requests your presence," she began. "They've called an urgent meeting regarding the princess." Inell lowered her gaze and watched the floor as if something there caught her attention. "I worry for Shahzar, Bishop. Please convince her to end this drive for revenge."

He followed the servant through the streets and up the steps that led to the castle's entry. Raynier felt frightened. The woman that returned from the wastelands was an imposing memory, a vengeful warrior. That the council would call on him to stop her proved a strange move indeed.

Raynier took his seat among the council members. Both Shahzar and Shahmi's seats remained vacant. The young foot-soldier that had brought back the captain's body and dressed Shahzar in her armor stood beside Sheah, the council's speaker.

"There are two matters we must resolve." Sheah knocked on the table with her stick. "The first is the matter of a new captain of the guards. Irlecain has come forward with the princess's wishes to take Shahmi's place. He's been among the soldiers all his life. He brought back Shahmi's body. Does anyone oppose his assignment to be captain?"

Silence.

"Then, so be it. Irlecain, take your place at that seat, and become a part of our council." Her words echoed with finality.

Irlecain sat beside Raynier and stared forward. The bishop watched the new captain pinch the back of his hand. He looked too young to be in such a prominent position. Under the scars and the defiant glare, there remained the face of a boy.

Sheah knocked on the table once more. "The second matter." Her brown eyes grazed each council member, indicating the severity of what was to come. She stared at Raynier last, holding his gaze as she spoke. "The princess keeps one last prisoner. She wears the key to his chamber around her neck and lets no one attend him. It's been four days that she's kept this Klemish man in seclusion. She did not come to this meeting, though we requested her presence. The matter must be resolved so I need your advice." Her eyes remained trained on Raynier as if she spoke only to him.

Irlecain stood up. His voice cracked, further attesting to his youth. "Princess Shahzar is with the man that killed her uncle!"

Sheah nodded, not at all surprised. "What happened that would make her act this way?"

"The man tortured Shahmi. Shahzar..." He cleared his throat, suddenly realizing the familiarity with which he'd just addressed her. "I mean to say, the princess told me that she wants the man to suffer as Shahmi did."

Eschelle stood. "This is not our way! We must force the door and take the man from her for execution—like the others! We do not torture prisoners. That is the Klemish way!"

Horlan stood as well. "I agree with Eschelle!" he barked.

One by one, the others stood and approved. Sheah nodded. "Irlecain," the speaker asked. "What do you propose we do?"

"I think we should allow Shahzar to do as her heart wills. The man is evil and deserves to die by her hand in whatever manner she deems fit." He crossed his arms over his chest, daring anyone to argue with him.

Horlan let out a long, impatient breath.

Sheah rapped at the table. "Bishop, you haven't spoken. Please stand and tell us what, if anything, you propose."

Raynier stood. He could feel all their eyes on him, waiting. He thought of Shahzar, carrying his child, torturing some man in a dark, stinking chamber and his stomach turned. "Let me speak to her."

"She will see no one but her chambermaid." The speaker's face relaxed, the dimples over her brows fading. "Go with Inell to see if she will admit you."

He nodded and took his leave. Inell, as if she'd known what would come of the meeting, waited beyond the council room in the archway. She escorted Raynier through the dim halls that led to Kaladia's dungeons. Soon the bishop found himself outside the door to a chamber that smelled more rank than he could ever imagine. It used to be a room for one of the prison wardens, but Shahzar had taken it over.

Inell spoke through the crack of the door. "Princess, Bishop Raynier has come to see you." From within, the key turned. The door opened a crack and swung wide. The servant pushed him into the darkness.

Shahzar slid the lock behind him. He stared up at the man she'd dragged from the desert, through the city streets and into this room. He was naked. Raynier found that shameful, but there were worse things. Tight shackles held the man against the wall. There were wounds from his neck to his feet, thin slices in his skin, which bled slowly, dribbling into the pool of blood on the floor beneath him. His chin rested on his chest. The bishop couldn't tell if he was conscious, but the tortured Klemish man still breathed steadily.

"What are you doing?" Raynier choked out. He looked away, tried to focus on the tiny window on the side wall. The sparse light it let in gave him a sense of hope.

When he turned, Shahzar sat down on the straw-covered floor in front of the prisoner. She crossed her legs and resembled any other weary foot-soldier that may have come home after a long battle.

Raynier sat down beside her and tried not to look at the blood. "Why are you doing this?"

Three weapons lay on the floor in front of her: her uncle's sword, her own dagger and another dagger etched with Klemish writings. She turned and focused her gaze on Raynier. "This man killed my uncle," she said in a calm voice. "This man made the mistake of telling me how he killed him, how long it took for him to die. He described in great detail Shahmi's suffering. I'm showing him how it feels to suffer like that. I'll kill him in the same way."

The coldness in her eyes appeared complete. Hatred burned within her. For a moment, Raynier thought there would be no way to stop her. He took her hand and whispered low so that the prisoner couldn't hear. "This isn't the Kaladian way. The council wants to execute him. Let it be so. Don't let this man's evil become part of you."

She pulled away and stood. Shahzar took a fistful of the prisoner's hair, a long tail that hung from the top of his head, and jerked his face up. "Do you know him?" She paused, waiting for an answer. "Look closely. Do you know this man?"

The prisoner's face lay mottled with runes. Whole phrases in Klemish scored his cheeks in tattoos. More ran down the bridge of his nose, even across his chin. His eyes cracked open. Raynier gasped at how black his pupils were and how, even in their darkness, they sparkled with cruelty.

The prisoner spat at the bishop's feet. "You bring me a priest?" he asked, his voice thick with a Klemish accent. He spoke as though the myriad of wounds he bore caused him no pain.

"Tell me, Raynier, do you know who this man is?" Shahzar asked. "Even Cain did not know."

"No," he answered. What did it matter who he was?

"He's their king! Tustin Aberweir, the king of Klem!" She pulled at the man's hair to jerk his face up higher.

"Even your priests are fools," the prisoner whispered.

She took up her dagger, the very blade that had waited under her pillow to end Raynier. She held it to the man's throat. "And who am I?" She hissed cold and deadly, glaring into his black eyes.

"A foot-soldier, nothing more. A woman at that. Untie my hands and I'll show you what good you are." He sneered at the princess.

"Who is the fool, now?" She growled. "Does your wife love you?"

"My wife?" His thin, black eyebrows creased.

"Yes, your queen, the queen of Klem. What is her name?"

The man seemed confused. "Ashandera," he muttered, his brows pressing even closer to one another.

Shahzar ran the tip of her dagger from Tustin's forehead to his chin, drawing a straight, bloody line. He didn't flinch, used to her torture by then. "Does your queen, your Ashandera, love you?"

"No." Tustin spoke with finality and, Raynier noticed, a certain malice for the questions Shahzar presented. It amazed the bishop that Tustin showed no sign of pain. His black eyes remained fixed on the princess. A pale light showed in her eyes.

"Why should I let you live? How could anyone love someone as vile as you with no regard for life?" she spat.

"My son will avenge me." Tustin spoke from the throes of a trance, mesmerized by that light in his captor's eyes. His voice lacked the conviction of his prior words.

"Let him come. I'll kill him too." She held the blade to his throat.

Raynier turned away from all the blood. He had no desire to look on the face of death. King Aberweir's last breath broke the silence with a wet, gurgling sound. The shadows danced in the dark corners of the chamber.

Their unnatural movement made his skin crawl. He glanced over his shoulder at the princess.

Shahzar's dagger fell. It dropped into the puddle of blood and more dribbled down from the dead man's fatal wound, coating the metal. "There, it's done. I've killed my enemy. His blood will be on my hands for all time."

She reached for Raynier. Her fingers caught the edge of his robes, and he turned fully just in time to catch her. Her skin felt icy; her eyelids drooped from days without sleep. "I'm cold as death," she whispered. "My uncle is speaking to me. He's there, behind you. Shahmi says you're a good man and that I should love no one else. But my uncle would never say such things..."

Raynier carried her out of the dungeon. Over Inell's protests, he carted the princess through the long, arched halls, all the way to her bedroom.

Shahzar slept against him, shivering until his warmth took away her chill. She mumbled in her sleep, her words the ghosts of old conversations she'd had with her uncle. Only once did she wake screaming that night. She sat upright in the middle of the bed, a slew of curses spewing past her lips, her eyes wide with fury, her hands clenched and held high, ready to strike.

"Shahzar," Raynier cried over her voice. "I'm here! You're safe in your bed!"

She crumpled and crawled on all fours to him. "I'm so cold," she murmured. "So cold when you're not here. I feel the city...breathing...every sound in the night..."

He held out his arms and she collapsed against his body. What she said made no sense. *Maybe she was having a nightmare*, he decided. He could only hold her and hope it passed.

In the morning, the two got up and sang the morning prayers. When their shared words ended and Raynier reached for her hand, Shahzar pulled away. "Send someone in your stead to the council meetings after this day," she ordered.

"Why?" His hand dropped to his side. Disappointment lined his face.

"I can only hurt you now," she replied. "I don't want to, but it will happen. Go back to the temple and become the bishop with all your heart. Forget me." The light left her eyes, replaced by a terrible, black emptiness.

Her words stung him. Raynier wanted to argue, wanted to ask for one more night, anything except this banishment from her, but Shahzar only guided him to the door and pushed him away.

Chapter Fourteen: Fealty to the Queen

Riel rode through the gates of Klem alone just as the morning sun peeked over the horizon. He looked down at the road, his heart heavy with guilt over his abandonment. No one questioned the captain as he passed through the merchant strip because he'd dressed himself as a shepherd. *I am no longer a soldier. I will keep my promise.* The camel he'd traded for in the herder settlement walked at a leisurely pace. Its tawny, blonde head bobbed from side to side, and he suspected the beast never saw a day of war in its life.

The guards at the castle gates stopped him. They stalked toward Riel with searching gazes. He hated to do it, but he pulled his facial covering down. "I have news for the queen," he called as the guards grabbed his camel's reins.

Both men bowed, recognizing the king's high captain. They parted in a flurry of azure cloaks to let him pass. Riel studied their gleaming silvery armor. He held back his smile. "Never again," he mumbled as he moved through. His days of fighting were over. The gods must have sent that 'thing' that attacked his regiment. The captain took it as a sign, a warning that the days for war should end. No one saw him flee because no one stood close enough in the darkness when he sidestepped the sword-wielding monster and let it take Tustin. He shook away the memory and kept moving.

The servants received him in the courtyard outside the barracks, one whisking his scrawny mount away to the stables and two more ready to attend to his needs. The captain waved the young boys away. He paused in the courtyard, his gaze wandering to the domed rooftop that peeked over the garden wall. "Home," he sighed. "Euphenia." He rubbed his chin, mulling over his next action.

A deep, defiant voice screamed across the practice yard. Riel spun on his heels, startled at how much it sounded like Tustin's and yet, it couldn't be. He squinted at the two trainees parrying in the circle. Once more, the young man yelled at his opponent and he cringed when Lochnar, Tustin's son, cracked his rattan shinai across the back of the other boy's legs.

"Low move," Riel muttered to himself. "You're just like your father." He shook his head at the prince's antics.

Lochnar's opponent fell to the dusty earth, clutching his legs and crying out in pain. Riel made up his mind that moment. He spared a final glance at the rooftop in the garden and headed for the barracks. "I've had enough of this cruelty," he muttered under his breath.

He approached his cousin's blocky house in the barrack quarter. That D'atham had not climbed in the ranks did not disprove his capabilities. The burly, bald man served with loyalty; he worked as hard as any high ranking official. His downfall had been that he chose the queen's side. His choice, he now knew, proved wise. A hammer pounding against metal echoed between the close buildings. He walked the small alley to the back of the squared, earth-plastered barrack, placing his hands on his hips to watch his cousin.

D'atham sat hunched over a near-finished wooden table, pounding the last nails into place. He looked solemn, his brow furrowed in concentration and his mouth a straight line with the final nail hanging from its corner. D'atham grasped the nail from his mouth, set it in place and hammered it in. He stood, surveying his work for a moment and righted the table, smiling.

"I've news, Cousin," Riel called.

D'atham looked up, startled. He crossed the distance between them in three wide steps and embraced the captain. "Good news, I hope." He stepped back and inspected his relative with concerned eyes.

"It is good news for your queen." He frowned, watching D'atham put both hands on his hips to hear what came next.

"We set upon Kaladia, killing villagers in the night. When their soldiers came against us, we retreated to the wastelands. Tustin lurked in the dunes, contemplating another attack, one to burn the Shan-Sei temple when the Kaladians came upon our camp. We defeated them."

D'atham nodded, taking in the small victory.

"Then, not a month later, something came at us in the darkness. It killed the mercenaries, the foot-soldiers. I don't think it was human. The demon came for Tustin..." Riel trailed off, unable to meet his cousin's deep, brown eyes.

Beyond the barracks, he heard Lochnar shouting, throwing his weight around and belittling the newer recruits. Shinais cracked against each other and a group of older men marched down the brick street, passing D'atham's home.

"The king is dead?" Riel's cousin guessed.

"I didn't try, that is..." He sucked in a breath. "Yes. Tustin Aberweir is dead."

D'atham smiled. He ran his meaty hand over his bald scalp and nodded. "And his brother? Did the demon in the sands kill that leach too?"

"Dalin had gone on patrol the day before. So no. I didn't see him, although..." He cleared his voice and looked down at his boots. "I must admit, Cousin, that I didn't go back to look."

"What are you saying, Riel?" D'atham asked. "Has my young cousin finally seen the error of his ways?"

"Daumion showed me the light in Kaladia. They are the same as we are. One people divided by an old war that our children will forget." He raised his gaze, no longer embarrassed by what he'd done. He met D'atham's strong-willed face with a stern look. "I must go to Ashandera. I have promised to serve her, but Cousin, I cannot fight anymore. My days in the ranks are over."

D'atham lunged forward and embraced his cousin tighter. "Euphenia will be happy to hear of it. You shower her with gifts she tells me she does not need."

"Stop keeping company with my wife," he grumbled as D'atham pulled away.

"If you stay at her side, my time with her beauty will be sacrificed." D'atham pouted, a comical expression on such a mighty looking man. "Come, let me take you to Zodrian. The queen will see you with his approval."

-o.O.o-

D'atham stood outside the ornate double doors to wait. Riel gave his cousin a dark look. Though he assumed the queen despised her husband, he still did not look forward to delivering the news of his death.

The old advisor, dressed in his amethyst colored robe and twisting a lock of his graying hair, beckoned Riel to enter. Zodrian muttered to himself, but Riel could not catch a word of what the elder said. The captain bypassed the frail man and knelt at Ashandera's bedside.

"Zodrian tells me you have news of my husband," she said.

Riel gazed up at his queen. This time no gauze curtains draped around her bed to obscure his view. She appeared much the same as she did the last time he saw her. Ashandera's face appeared sunken, her eyes too deep-set and her mouth drawn in a tired expression. Her brown skin looked too yellowed, a side-effect of whatever poison Tustin offered her as a wedding gift. The queen's eyes remained fixed across the room at the window.

"The Kaladians attacked us in the wastelands," Riel stated. "King Aberweir was captured. Rumors spread that the Kaladian queen tortured and executed him."

Ashandera remained still a long while, her gaze empty and stuck on the one point that interested her. Riel decided she watched the window with longing. *Maybe she wants to cast her dying body through it and be done with her lingering death.* Riel turned and studied the glass as well. He did not turn back until he heard her sniffle. Tears ran down her sallow cheeks and more pooled in her brown eyes, spilling forth.

"I'm sorry, my queen," Riel announced. He knew he should lie then, that he should tell her he tried to save Tustin, but he could not bring himself to do it. So he told Ashandera something closer to the truth. "I have failed you. Please allow me to leave the army and serve out the rest of my days in shame."

"Shame," the queen repeated. At last, she turned on him, a sickening sorrow reflecting in her gaze. Her lower lip trembled. "I am shamed more so by what I let that man do. Go and retire if that is your wish, Captain." She settled back into her purple pillows and closed her eyes. The queen pushed her hands under her blankets.

"My queen, if I may. There is one more thing I ask of you." He maintained his position on the floor, humble at her side like a devout servant. "My cousin, D'atham, has always been loyal to you. He serves in the army as a tracker, but I think you might find his allegiance to you and his abilities in battle make him worthy of a higher rank."

Ashandera's eyes cracked open, a look of disgust curling her lips. "What's this? You tell me my husband is dead and ask that I promote your cousin?"

"I beg you, my queen. He will protect you with his life. There is no man more steadfast to you than D'atham." Riel looked over his shoulder and saw his cousin in the hall, his eyes wide with surprise. He turned back to the queen, praying that she would take him. "Your husband passed him over for promotion five times because he would not renounce his fealty to you."

Ashandera craned her head to the side, trying to see the other man in the hall. She squinted and raised one thin, skeletal hand, beckoning D'atham to enter. "This is your cousin?" she whispered.

"Yes, my queen."

D'atham came forward. He stood beside his kneeling cousin and gently kicked Riel's boot. "What are you doing?" he whispered between clenched teeth.

He looked up at him and sighed. "I swear to you, he is loyal. There is no man more deserving of a promotion than my cousin."

The queen's eyes rolled over D'atham's shape. She scooted forward, slow, unsteady, and evidenced by her slight moan, in some degree of pain. Her straight, black hair fell across her face and she let it hang there. "What position do you desire for your cousin, Captain Riel?"

Riel paused, unsure. "Captain," he said with finality.

Ashandera held out her hand to D'atham. The large man knelt on both knees and took her fingers gently in his own. He pressed the queen's palm to his forehead in an act of loyalty. "My cousin is a fool, good queen," he said. "Forgive him. He asks too much of you in this time of mourning. I am content to serve you as a tracker."

Riel noticed a smile spreading across Ashandera's lips. D'atham could not possibly see it bent over as he was. In that moment, he felt sure that she would promote his cousin.

"Rise, Tracker. I have need of honest men." Her fingers slipped through D'atham's. Ashandera turned her head back to the arched window, her eyes glossing over and the same smile curling her lips.

Chapter Fifteen: Memories

Five months later, Raynier walked up the marble steps to her room, his heart thundering in his chest. Inell sent word in the middle of the night that their child arrived. He knocked softly on Shahzar's door. It took a long time for Inell to answer, and when she did, Raynier smiled at her familiar, bulging eyes. "Are they well?" he asked.

The servant shrugged and stood aside so the bishop could enter. He walked across the green rug, much as he had the first time he'd come to her room. The ornate furnishings drew his attention. New gold bed-curtains replaced the green ones. The lighter color and the fact that they'd been tied back to the posts gave her bedchamber an open feel. Shahzar slept against the pillows, her long, black hair twisted into a braid that hung over her shoulder. Raynier sat at the edge of the bed and stared down at her face.

After several long moments, he looked over at the baby, asleep in the crook of Shahzar's arm. The infant lay swaddled in a soft, azure-colored blanket that revealed only the child's brown skin. A few curls of black hair peeked from the edge of the blanket. The baby had thick, black eyelashes. "Is it a boy?" he whispered.

"Yes," said Inell, a touch of sadness in her voice. "The council has decided to foster him to the family of a foot-soldier to be raised as such."

In his heart, Raynier rejoiced. Ishas had answered his prayers. In time, the rite must take place once more. Maybe then, she would look on him with favor. Without a daughter, there could be no future queen.

Inell reached down to take the child. Shahzar shot up like a frightened animal and clutched the baby back before the servant even lifted him.

"I'll change his wrap now, milady," she explained.

Shahzar's gilt-brown eyes focused. Her fingers trembled. She gazed shiftily from Raynier back to Inell. "No! You can't take him from me. He's mine!"

Inell backed away, familiar with Shahzar's outbursts. "His wraps are on the table, milady. I'll leave you alone now, if you wish."

"Yes! Go! Get out and let me sleep." Shahzar held her head up, her eyes narrowed on Inell until the servant finally left. When the door closed, she leaned back and sighed. "The council will not decide his fate. He's mine. He's the one, true heir. I won't have my son forced into the guard. That's what they did to Shahmi." Her voice caught in her throat at the mention of her uncle's name. She sucked in a heavy breath and turned, at last, to look at the bishop. "Raynier," she said, forcing a weak smile. "You have a son."

"He's beautiful, like his mother." He moved close, a peculiar feeling washing over him. He wanted to touch their child, to touch her, to know the joy of having a family. To want those things went against tradition. Bittersweet regret over his position and Shahzar's twisted his heart. His family would be forever distant.

She nodded, her lips pursed. It took effort, but she scooted upright and held out the small infant to Raynier. "You are the first to hold him. Inell keeps trying, but I wanted to wait for you."

The bishop cradled the bundle, nervously. He'd never held a child so young before that day. The baby's tiny, dark eyes opened. He blinked at his father. The infant looked like an ancient man who'd been woken unjustly from a peaceful nap.

"His name is Al-Shamah," Shahzar announced. "It's Old Kaladian for The Sun."

"It's a beautiful name," he said, still staring at his son. For once, with Shahzar present, Raynier found an object of adoration and intrigue besides her.

"You will see him whenever you like." She placed her hand on his shoulder for a moment, the meaning of what she'd said hanging in the air.

"It is forbidden," Raynier mumbled as he studied her face. It went against the old ways to be allowed to see the child and be offered such a right as fatherhood.

"I do not forbid it." Weariness edged hers serene expression.

Raynier nodded. He had no desire to argue with her. She offered him the chance to be a father, to be part of his child's life, a gift he never thought he'd be given. "And you?" he asked. "Did the birth go as it should?"

"They said it went well. I've walked across the room already. I just feel so...tired." She reached over and laid her hand on Raynier's knee. "I'm afraid to sleep, afraid they'll take him from me," she whispered.

"Nonsense, Shahzar." He set the baby beside her. "Do you want me to stay with you? Watch over you while you sleep?" In truth, he wanted that and he felt certain, even in her state, that she knew his desires.

Surprisingly, she nodded and turned on her side, resigned to his care. Her eyes slipped shut and her face relaxed. Her breathing deepened within minutes. Raynier kept vigil over her through the night. When their son woke for feedings, he stayed close by. When he needed his wraps changed, the bishop attempted, and finally mastered the mundane task. He watched over Shahzar just as he said he would.

In the morning, she pushed herself out of the bed. Raynier sat at the desk, the swaddled child fast asleep in his arms. "Get some more sleep," he told her. "Al-Shamah is fine. I just changed him."

"No," she said. "I take the throne this morning. I have born a child blessed by the temple. The crown is mine now." She walked to the door in slow, weary steps, pried it open a crack and peered out. "Inell! Come and dress me."

In minutes, the servant came bounding in, her face flushed at the request. "Milady, are you certain you shouldn't wait?" she asked, tucking her veil behind her ear. "The healers said you should rest."

"I want the ceremony to take place this morning." Shahzar clung to the bedpost and waited. "Dress me. I will carry my child to the throne and claim my title. My day has finally come."

About the Author

Anastasia Rabiyah writes erotic romance, paranormal erotic romance, and fantasy. She often crosses genres in order to follow her muses into the darkness where they seek out destiny in all its forms. She believes in fairies, demons, angels, magic, passion, chocolate, supportive friends, e-books and writing critique groups. Her deepest desire is to pursue her creative dreams and realize them. Every spare moment she devotes to writing for her haunting muses.

Visit her on the web at:

RabiyahBooks.com

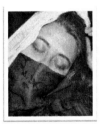

Follow Your Dreams!